The
TWELVE
SWIPES
of
CHRISTMAS

First paperback edition November 2022

Cover by Enni Tuomisalo

Edited by Jennifer Safrey

ISBN 979-8-9865455-0-9 (paperback)

ISBN 979-8-9865455-1-6 (ebook)

For my husband who won't stop telling people I wrote a book.

One

I pride myself on my extensive vocabulary. Not to toot my own horn, but I did have one of the highest GPAs in my graduating class. However, when I grab my phone off the couch cushion and swipe to open the new notification, I am truly speechless.

"What has you looking all bug-eyed?" my roommate and best friend Mila asks.

My facial expression doesn't waver as I turn the screen toward her so she can see what she's done to me.

A moment of silence passes between us before she tilts her head. "I don't get it. Is that a—"

"Tattoo on someone's dick?" I practically shout. "Yeah. Thanks to you and your need to get me on these stupid dating apps, I'm now getting photos of penis tattoos sent to me."

"You've gotten more than one?"

My stare turns cold and she bites the inside of her cheek to keep from laughing.

"This is the eighth guy I've talked to. Now, it's the first *tattooed* genital picture I've received, but this is getting exhausting."

She giggles, "Well, you had MeetCute open on your phone. I just figured you could use a little push. An early Christmas present, if you will."

My eyes narrow at her. "It's only Black Friday. You're the one who insists I'm not allowed to even think about Christmas until December first. That's still" — I look at my wrist, pretending to check a watch that isn't there — "nine days away."

Christmas will always hold a special place in my heart. In my opinion, the second everyone is done overeating turkey, stuffing, and mashed potatoes, it's time to put up the tree. Mila complained it was too early to decorate when I first brought the tree up from storage a week ago, so I've just been getting very comfortable with our fake pine in my room. And, yes, it kills me to admit I have a fake tree, but I had to compromise with my roommate on a few things. Mila has been my person for as long as I can remember, but she can only take my holiday craziness (her words, not mine) for so long.

"Like you aren't enjoying the attention. Plus, it's time for you to get back on the horse. Johnny left four months ago—"

I cross my arms and raise an eyebrow, trying to convey this is a dangerous slope she should stay far far away from. "You are not seriously bringing up my ex to convince me online dating is a good idea, are you?"

Placing her hands up defensively, she says, "This is supposed to be fun. Maybe you find Mr. Right, or maybe you find Mr. Right Now. Either way, the purple rabbit in your nightstand needs a break."

My mouth drops in horror. Are the walls really that thin?

"Yes, the walls are really that thin," she responds, reading my thoughts. She tilts her head back, finishing the rest of her wine, then smiles.

"Trust me, I know how thin the walls are. Why do you think I bought noise-canceling headphones? You and Trey go at it like rabid animals. Last time I almost called the police because I thought one of you was murdering the other."

Mila props her elbow on the back of the couch, tangling her fingers in her hair with a ridiculously large smile on her face. "Oh, yeah. That was a good night."

Grabbing the throw pillow behind my back, I whip it at her face. She doesn't even try to stop it, just tosses her head back and laughs like a hyena. God, I love her.

I shake my head, turning my attention back to my phone. Seeing that I forgot to click out of the dick pic (why would someone ever get a tattoo down there?), I shut my eyes and frantically swipe, hoping it will disappear forever. A chuckle that is much deeper than Mila's fills the room and I open my eyes, sighing in relief at my home screen.

"Why are you acting weird today, Tater Tot?" Trey inquires as he enters the room. Trey, Mila's boyfriend who acts like he lives here, has been in my life almost as long as Mila has. He's probably one of my best guy friends, which is nice because when Mila tries to comfort me, Trey will instead give me the raw and dirty truth.

"You would act weird too if some random guy sent you a picture of his tattooed junk to try to get you into bed!"

Trey freezes mid-sitting down. "I feel like this is some girl-bonding shit that I don't need to be part of."

Mila grabs his shoulder, forcing him down next to her. "Tatum isn't as open to her Christmas present as I thought she would be."

"Is this what peer pressure feels like? I always thought it would happen to me in high school, not when I was a grown adult."

Trey nods a few times, a slow smile creeping across his face. "Right. The dating apps. I told her you wouldn't go for it." Trey reaches across Mila, grabbing my wine glass and taking a sip before I can object. His face pinches as he pretends to gag and sets the glass back down.

"Thank you!" I shout, tossing my hands in the air. "You know what? It's fine. I'm just going to delete them."

Mila's face falls as she sits up straight. "The hell you are! Give me that!"

She grabs for my phone and I pull it away just in time. When Mila's determined, it can get scary — and that fire in her eyes tells me I'm in trouble.

Within two seconds of my jumping off the couch, Mila snatches my phone. I gape as she sticks her tongue out at me.

"You really should make your password something other than 1111."

"That's not fair! Trey, do something!" I whine.

He just laughs, settling into his seat as I run after her but she quickly ducks and does a barrel roll to the other side of the room.

A shocked but impressed expression falls over my face. When the hell did she get so flexible?

She shrugs, answering my internal question again. "Yoga."

When she dares to look away, I run at full force and tackle her to the ground.

"Oh, shit!" Trey shouts, dropping to the floor next to us and hitting the ground the way referees do in pro wrestling matches. "One, two, three, the winner!"

He grabs my arm and raises it in victory. This results in us both laughing and groaning in pain as we roll onto our backs.

"I think we're getting old." I giggle while trying to catch my breath, praying I didn't dislodge a lung or something in the fall.

"We're only twenty-eight," Mila pants.

"Well, that's too old for this shit."

Mila sits up, runs a hand through her long dirty-blond hair, and smiles. "If I knew your present involved you tackling me, I would've done all this while you were sleeping." Then she turns her attention to her boyfriend, smacking him on the shoulder. "You dumbass, you're supposed to protect me. I am your girlfriend."

He leans forward, gently kissing her forehead. "Tater Tot," he says to me, "you're amazing, but I have no doubt Mila could kick your ass."

I nod, still trying to suck in oxygen. "Agreed."

Trey bends down, offering a hand to help me up after helping Mila. Once I'm fully vertical again, I brush my hair out of my face and aggressively steal my phone back.

"Fine." I sigh. "I won't delete them yet. But did you have to download four apps? Wasn't one enough?"

Mila's perfectly shaped brows pinch together. "I spent time researching these apps, and the four I downloaded are highly successful. And no one app is going to have all these great men. This is just us setting a wide trap and waiting to reel them in." Her voice reaches a new octave, which means she put a lot of thought into this. I know she wants me to have what she and Trey have. I thought I potentially could have that with Johnny until — nope, not going there.

I inhale sharply through my nose, exhaling slowly through my mouth. "Okay. Fine. Then tell me, Emilia, what the reasoning behind my profile picture is."

"Um, because you look hot," she says like it's so obvious. "And don't call me by my full name. You know I can't stand it."

Grabbing my phone out of my hand again, she pulls up said picture to show Trey.

He peers down at the screen. In the picture, Mila's long hair hangs in loose beachy waves down her back. Her green midi dress has a straight-neckline detail and a tulle bottom, making her look like a fairy. My shoulder-length brown hair was pinned half up, half down while my makeup is brown and smoky. Mila had picked out eyeshadows she said brought out my hazel eyes. I'm wearing a burgundy velvet off-the-shoulder dress that hugs all my curves and hits just above my knees, a small slit running up the thigh. Oh, and did I forget to mention the dress is a little too tight around my chest, so my boobs were practically hitting me in the face all night after we took the picture? The dress was gifted to me by Mila.

"Damn!" Trey says. "Now I see why someone sent you a dick pic."

I turn my death glare on Mila as she elbows Trey in the ribs. He grits his teeth, probably not wanting to admit that a five-foot-three girl can hurt him. He towers over her and if you didn't know he wouldn't, you would think he'd use his six-foot-one height to intimidate you. But everyone who knows Trey knows he is one big softie.

"I'm going to go smother my boyfriend," Mila says. "Please, just give it another chance? Oh, and block that last guy."

Mila grabs Trey's arm, dragging him down the hallway to her bedroom. I don't want to keep looking, but I guess it can't get much worse. Taking Mila's advice, I block the loser who sent me the unsolicited picture and move on.

My thumb hovers over the yellow icon with little white hearts called MeetCute. Six talk bubbles pop up, asking if I want to peruse profiles. The first one I click is named Alex. He's single (obviously), a dad, and has a dog. He says his little boy is the best thing that's ever happened to him. Well, isn't Alex freaking adorable? I click on his picture and start to scroll. He's tall and slender with a gap between his two front teeth. One of the pictures is of him and his son standing in front of a lake at sunset. If Mila is right and all of this does work out, maybe I could be standing in a picture like that one day. My mind changes pretty fast when I scroll down and find *"not having a conniving bitch of a wife"* under Favorite Hobbies.

Next.

Larry is a welder who is forty-four years old and has never been in a serious relationship before. He is looking for a woman who meets every single one of his standards, and he refuses to lower them. She must cook and clean and not work — as the man is supposed to provide everything. He actually wrote bullet points on what his future wife should look like.

I'm happy when I don't meet any of his expectations. Next.

The next three all say that they just got out of horrible relationships and want to bang every woman who responds to them. Ew. This is the exact reason I never tried online dating before. Creeps and assholes flood the internet, thinking everyone else is the problem. Clicking on the final guy, I sigh in relief. I'm not the kind of person who only thinks about physical appearance, but if I was, this guy would definitely be at the top of my list. Dark-brown styled hair paired with green eyes hidden under thick black lashes. Muscles I would possibly drool over if I ever got close enough to admire. Is that a tattoo peeking out from the bottom of his sleeve? I've never really been into bad boys, but something about tattoos gets me all excited. The non-genital kind. Nash is a thirty-one-year-old doctor looking for the right woman. He has a passion for helping people, working out, and his cat, Smelly Cat. I laugh out loud at the "Friends" reference.

Damn. Score one for Mila. Grabbing my glass off the coffee table, I gingerly sip the sweet wine as I debate what to do. I could respond and say how delicious he looks and that I want to eat sushi off his abs peeking through his tight thermal shirt. No, that would be weird. I could just say he seems interesting and I would love to get dinner with him. Or I could just ignore his message and delete the apps altogether. That last option was from the Grinch, who sometimes appears on my shoulder when I'm tired.

"This was a nice thing Mila did. Now, you be quiet," I tell him as I set my drink down and pick my phone back up.

Nash,

My name is Tatum, but you already know that from my profile. I would love to grab a cup of coffee or a drink with you sometime when you are free. What's your work schedule like?

Sent. Okay, that was surprisingly easy. On to app number two, BeeMine. Only three matches on this app, but that's okay because there's only one contender. Well, sort of. Brendon is a thirty-two-year-old architect looking for love in his life. He believes in fate and destiny and that is why he is currently single. He would love to take a nice woman out on the town and show off some of his favorite spots. I scroll through his pictures and can only think of one word. Adorable. Black-rimmed glasses over eyes so blue I want to swim in them with dirty blond hair carefully gelled into place. In his profile picture, he's wearing a grey peacoat with a black turtleneck underneath and he's laughing at something just out of frame.

"Okay, fine. Mila gets two points," I mumble to myself as I send Brendon a message. Shockingly, I send out three more messages before I finish going through my notifications. LoveLanguage has only one option that interests me. Beau is twenty-nine-years-old and is loving life. He is an accountant who loves to travel and experience new things. DateMe produces Cole. He is twenty-eight years old and loves to play his guitar, which he named Shelly. He was in a band in college, but now just plays whenever he has the time. He wants to find a woman he can serenade to the altar.

Completely exhausted after sending the messages, I debate going to bed. Then I realize it's only eight o'clock. My shoulders slump as I think I am the lamest twenty-eight-year-old out there. I down the rest of my wine during my little pity party, then decide I don't care and stand up. As I'm walking back to my room, it's suspiciously quiet and part of me wonders if Mila did smother Trey. I shrug and turn towards my room, flipping the light switch on. Forgetting that a giant tree bag is taking up a portion of my room, I groan in pain when I walk right into it.

"Nine more days," I mutter.

My phone vibrates in my hand. It's from Nash, but I don't know if I have the mental capacity to deal with more dirty pictures tonight. I toss my phone on my nightstand and get ready for bed. After washing my face, brushing my teeth, and changing into my PJs, curiosity gets the better of me.

Tatum,

I would love to grab a drink with you. I just got off a double shift, so tonight might not be the best idea. I wouldn't want your first impression to be me falling asleep at the table. How about tomorrow night? I'll meet you at Sunny's at 8? Just so you know, we doctors don't always wear our white coats. Instead, I'll be in a black sports coat. I look forward to meeting you.

Nash.

Two

- -

Sunny's, a local bar hidden in a small neighborhood in the East End of Pittsburgh, is only a few blocks from my house. I'm a tad impressed he knows the place. The best part is the drinks are cheap enough to keep you drinking all night, but strong enough to put you on your ass if you're not careful.

Stepping over the threshold, I scan the crowd for Nash. I'm not sure why, considering I have no idea what he looks like. I mean, I saw his picture on his profile, but he could look different in real life. The idea of potentially getting catfished flashes through my brain. I swear, if that's what's happening, I'm filling Mila's Christmas stocking with Trey's gross gym socks. With the long wooden bar to my left and booths to my right, I continue my search.

You know how in the movies, the lonely girl makes eye contact with the incredibly hot doctor, and they feel some kind of instant connection? As crazy as it sounds, I think that just happened to me. The insanely attractive man I've been messaging is smiling his adorable lopsided smile back at me. The hair on the back of my neck stands on end as his eyes travel the length of my body. Since it technically isn't December, Mila said it was too early to wear my Christmas-themed clothes. Instead, I chose dark denim skinny jeans, an off-the-shoulder sweater, and black heeled boots. I did manage to grab my candy cane earrings before I ran out the door. Standing up, he buttons his sports coat before approaching me. My breathing slows as I take in his large athletic frame and I forget to swallow for a minute.

"Tatum?" His eyebrows raise like he's hoping it's me.

I nod, unable to speak. "Uh-huh. That's me. Tatum. You're Nash, right?"

A husky chuckle falls from his lips. "That's me. Can I buy you a drink?"

Nash places his hand in the middle of my back before guiding me to a booth in the corner of the room. Tripping over my boots, I force a smile and slide onto the splitting black leather while Nash sits opposite me. Neither of us says anything for at least thirty seconds and I'm not sure if it's because he's trying to not make fun of my clumsiness or there's just nothing to say.

Now I remember why I don't go on blind dates.

Nash clears his throat. "Tatum, what kind of drinks do you like?"

"Something with booze," I say before thinking. That probably makes me sound like I have a problem, so I decide to nervously laugh. "I meant, since we're at a bar... "

I let my sentence trail off while I grab the drink menu sitting to the right of me. I'm such a mess. I'll be surprised if he can even make it through one drink with me.

A tall blond with a scowl appears at our table. "Orders?"

"Scotch on the rocks for me and the lady will have... "

"Um, I guess I'll just have a cranberry vodka."

"How original," I hear the waitress mumble as she walks away and I frown.

"So, tell me about yourself," Nash starts.

"Well, I am a writer and I live with my best friend, and somehow she convinced me to go on a dating app." More nervous laughter.

Nash runs his long fingers through his thick tousled hair that I itch to touch. "Yeah, dating apps can be kind of weird. I've met a few women who looked nothing like their profiles and then would tell me how I was stupid for putting my information out on the internet."

"Right? At least it's not just me who is nervous—"

"No reason to be nervous. Just a fun date between two adults." His smile has my entire face heating up.

"What's your last name?" I blurt.

He chuckles. "Anderson. Nash Anderson. And yours?"

"My what?" Is my voice shaking? Why am I so damn nervous?

His smile is soft and comforting. "Your last name."

"Oh. Right. That. Moore. Tatum Moore." I sit there, staring at his face that seems too perfect to be real. "Okay, your turn. What about you and your life?"

"Well, I am a doctor at St. Margaret's. I work in the Emergency Department and the reason I am on a dating app is that it is very difficult to date with my hours. Too busy saving lives and kissing babies."

My brows pinch together. I can't tell if he's joking or if he's the arrogant doctor stereotype.

Choosing to ignore his comment, I hold up my drink the waitress just dropped off and we clink our glasses together.

"Working in the Emergency Department must be insane. I bet you see some crazy stuff," I say before taking a drink of my way-too-sweet drink.

"It can be, but I assure you it's nothing like television makes it out to be. Sorry, but is something wrong with your drink?"

I didn't realize my eye was twitching. "It's fine."

I take another drink and do my best to smile.

"I can get you another drink if that one is too sweet or too sour." Nash is about to stand when I grab his wrist.

"I said it's fine. I like it. Really." Why do guys always think I can't speak up for myself? I mentally roll my eyes, praying I'm not on a date with another Johnny.

With an expression that tells me he isn't convinced, Nash sits back down. I just don't like being that person who has to complain about everything when I go out.

"All right."

More silence. Shit, I just made things awkward. I guess it was sweet of him to want to get me another drink, but I'm capable of getting another one myself.

"Any fun stories from the hospital?" I ask, trying to change the subject.

Nash leans closer to me. "Please let me get you another drink. It's silly to just sit here and sip on something you don't like."

Why are we still talking about this? To get it through his head that I do not want another drink, I bring the glass to my lips and take a large gulp. Nash's jaw clenches as the liquid burns the entire way down my esophagus.

"Yum. I told you, I don't need another." I'm about to try to segue into a different topic when I catch him rolling his eyes. "I'm sorry, did you just roll your eyes at me?"

At first, he looks like a kid who was caught with his hand in the cookie jar but then he exhales sharply. "You know what? I did roll my eyes at you."

"What is your problem?"

Nash rubs his fingers on his temples like I'm exhausting him or something. Through gritted teeth he mutters, "Look, we came out tonight and I paid for a service. The service was not up to standard, and I just think we should remedy that. It's not a big deal to ask for a new drink. I figured that as an adult, you would know how to speak up for yourself. Look, I'm sure the bartender wouldn't mind."

Crossing my arms, I say, "And I said I don't need a new one. God, why are all men the same?"

He opens his mouth and I hold my hand up. "That was a rhetorical question. And you're wrong about one thing."

"What's that, sweetheart?" Nash says with the most condescending attitude I've ever heard.

Pushing myself out of the booth, I stand and toss a ten-dollar bill on the table. "You didn't pay for shit."

I'm about to walk away when I realize I have one more thing left to say. "Just so you know, I didn't send the drink back because I am nice enough to realize that some people make mistakes. It's not a big deal and if it wasn't for you being rude, I would've enjoyed my drink."

Still enraged, I pick up my drink and dump the rest of its contents in Nash's lap before leaving.

Thank God Mila let me borrow her car so I have a quick escape. Stomping through the snow, I try my best to take deep, calming breaths. How unbelievably arrogant was that guy? He acted exactly as I thought a doctor would act: full of himself. Just because he can save lives doesn't mean he is the most desired man in the world. My entire body shakes when I remember I thought he was hot. Gross! Slamming the door, I turn on the Camry and crank the heat up as high as it will go.

I can't believe I just went on a date with another guy who thinks the world should bow down to him. Pulling my phone out of my purse, I instantly delete MeetCute. It did not live up to its name. My thumb hovers over the other three dating apps. The icons shake as if they're nervous they are next. I should just delete them all and tell Mila that I gave her present a try but it didn't work out.

It was very sweet of Mila to think of me. I guess just because Nash was the biggest, most arrogant person I have ever met doesn't mean every guy on a dating app will be. I need to keep an open mind. As much as I hate to admit it, Mila is right and I would love to share the holidays with someone. I mean, she and Trey are great, but it's kind of awkward to be the third wheel during a holiday. Last year, they invited me to go ice skating with them and I thought it was a great idea. Instead, they held hands the entire time while I struggled to stand on the ice. I ended up falling and somehow slicing my finger with my own skate. Four stitches and I haven't looked at an ice rink since. Letting out a loud groan, I click my phone shut and drive.

The car bumps up and down on the old-time brick street as I pull away. That mixed with the art and music that appear around every corner and the incredible views make the "City of Bridges" home.

When I finally make it into the house, I'm more annoyed than upset. I can't believe I wasted my night. I could've stayed at home, snuggled under my weighted blanket, and watched *America's Next Top Model* while eating an obscene amount of junk food. Once inside, a quick scan of our rustic-themed living room tells me either Mila and her boo have retired to her room, or they aren't here. Either way, I plan on taking a hot shower, getting in bed, and forgetting this night ever happened.

My alarm goes off three times before I finally manage to get out of bed. When I catch a glimpse of myself in the mirror on the back of my door, I almost jump in horror at the person staring back at me. Dark eyes, crazy hair, and a stress zit on my chin that has appeared overnight. When I finally emerge from my room, I find Mila's door still closed. She's usually up before me, so I knock to make sure she's alive before heading to the kitchen. As I'm making my morning coffee, Mila and Trey stumble in, wearing each other's shirts.

"Was this an accident or some new style I haven't heard of?" I tease.

Mila ignores me while Trey looks down at the insanely tight pink V-neck that reads "Hugs, Not Drugs." With a loud groan, he stomps back down the hallway.

"Someone looks like they had a fun night," I say as I grab another mug out of the cabinet for Mila. She practically tackles me to get her hands on some caffeine.

"Thanks for this." She holds the mug tightly as she inhales the aroma. After a long gulp, she sighs happily. "Trey brought over some whiskey last night and we drank way too much. I haven't been this hungover since college."

I am forced to bite my lip so I don't laugh directly in her face. Mila has always been a lightweight and it's only gotten worse since we graduated. Sipping from my mug, I watch her eyes flutter shut like she is debating falling back asleep while sitting at the kitchen table.

"Maybe you should use your sick day. It wouldn't be a total lie."

She nods before stopping immediately. "That was a mistake." Mila sloshes some coffee on the counter when she drops her mug and runs to the bathroom.

When my mug is empty, I refill it and head to our basement. Mila, being the most amazing friend ever, agreed that the downstairs could be my office. Our compromise was I could take over the entire room, but I had to let her spin bike stay in the corner. It works out because when I get stuck on a problem, I get on the bike as a distraction. The cream carpet with the gray walls and whitewashed brick fireplace is the perfect vibe for a writer. Sitting down at my desk, I power up my laptop and open my web browser. I start to open up *Starz Weekly,* the blog I write reviews for, but instead click on my Google Docs and look at one project in particular. Sadness spreads through me as I read "Last edit was 23 days ago."

Here's the thing. I have about a million ideas in my head and I would love to share them with people. What better way to do that than to write a book? Sounds simple, right? Not! I have been working on this particular project for more than two years. One of my friends from college, Allie, is also a writer and she's been helping me revise my story. Picture this: A man and a woman fall in love, only to find out that they were each other's childhood nemesis. Hilarity ensues and it's probably the cutest romantic comedy I've ever read. Okay, I may be a little biased.

My last edit was twenty-three days ago because that's when the ideas stopped coming to me. The book is finished, but I'm not satisfied with it. Once I think of a great and epic ending, then it will be done. However, it's as if a brick wall appeared in my brain and completely halted my creativity. As of last week, I have officially saved up enough money to cover the cost of self-publishing. Allie keeps checking in on me and asking how it's going, but I keep dodging her calls. I know I'm a horrible friend, but how can I call myself a writer when I'm not writing?

Shaking my empty head, I open up my bookmarked tab for *Starz Weekly*. The blog is kind of like a poor man's TMZ. The website struggled for the first year but has become majorly successful since. My job is to find trendy new blogs and review them on our site. It's as stupid and pointless as it sounds, but it pays the bills.

Three

"Okay, no joke. That was so close. Trey was trying to get into the bathroom at the same time as me and I almost had to bulldoze him to get to the toilet." Mila laughs to herself as she plops down in the beige chair on the other side of my desk.

"I take it no work, then?"

"Nada."

"Well, go watch TV or something because some of us still have to clock in. The only downside to working from home is that I can never call off." I groan.

"But if I go upstairs, how can I annoy you? Isn't that what best friends are for?"

I smile, then instantly frown when my eyes travel back to my computer screen.

"The current blog I'm being forced to look at is about how TikTok is the greatest achievement of our time. I swear to God, I'm losing IQ points reading this shit."

"No luck job hunting?" Mila asks. I know she means well, but it only makes me more grumpy. It's no secret I hate my job, but every job I'm interested in either wants you to have your Master's or pays way less than my current salary. If Mila and I lived in an apartment or even a townhouse, I could probably do that, but I can't stop paying my share of the mortgage. Adulthood unfortunately doesn't work like that.

Taking a calming breath, I say, "Job hunt is currently on pause. Nothing good right now."

I love Mila, but I'm hoping my short answer will get her out of here faster. One, I can't focus on this stupid blog with her here and two, I'm sure I know why she's down here and I don't want to talk about it.

"Mhm, okay, well ... What about last night?"

My eyes widen at the memory of Sunny's. The most incredibly awful first date. "Believe it or not, I've never poured a drink on someone's lap before."

"What?"

"Huh?" I pretend to start typing something, but Mila walks around my desk and pulls my chair away from the laptop. "Mila—"

"Oh, please. That stupid blog can wait. I want to hear about last night!" She starts to jump up and down before instantly regretting that action. Sometimes I wonder how such a big personality can fit into the tiny little package known as Mila.

"It was awful, okay? Can I please get back to work now?"

She looks hurt. "Not a chance! You can't just say something like that and expect me not to pry. I need details."

With a few grunts, Mila pulls the chair she was previously in closer to me. After sitting and making sure she's comfortable, she gestures for me to continue my story. I pinch the bridge of my nose, wishing I was still sleeping.

"It's not that I don't want to talk to you, it's just—I don't know. He was hot, but rude and a jerk. I ended the night by dumping my drink in his lap and leaving. Mila, I really do appreciate everything, but I don't think—"

"You dumped your drink in his lap? Oh my God! What did he do?" Her shrieks only get louder and I'm sure Trey can hear her from upstairs.

"Honestly, it was just something so simple. My drink wasn't that great, but I didn't want to send it back. He turned it into this big thing and became an asshole, so I left. I don't think dating apps are my thing."

"No, no, don't say that!" Mila says in a soothing tone as she tries to scoot her chair even closer to me. When it doesn't move, she rolls mine closer to her. Grabbing my hand, she looks directly into my eyes. "I love you so much, but you can't give up. Look, not all guys are going to be winners. Don't forget what my mom always said. You have to—"

"Kiss a couple of frogs to find your prince. I know, I know."

Mila's mom, Cindy, was like my second mom growing up. Since Mila was an only child, I almost felt like her sister. Being able to call her mom by her first name made it feel like she was just another friend. About three years ago, she lost her battle with cancer. Her passing made its way into the top five worst days of my life.

"Do it for Mom. You know she would love to see you find your happily ever after. Especially around Christmastime. It would be like a little Christmas miracle."

My mouth drops in shock. "You did not just play the dead mother card. That is so uncalled for."

We both start to giggle as I swat her arm.

"I'm serious. Didn't you say you connected with a few other guys?" When I nod, she continues, "Just go out with them and if they're all a total failure, I will stop hounding you."

"But—"

"Give them a chance. Remember when Trey hit on me before we were dating? He used that awful pick-up line."

I smile, remembering the exact moment she's talking about.

I deepen my voice to mimic Trey. "Aside from being sexy, what do you do for a living?"

We burst out laughing.

"He didn't even ask my name first," she recalls. "But I gave him another chance and now look at us."

I'm about to say something, put up more of a fight, but I just sigh. She's right. I shouldn't write off the entire male population just because of one dud.

"Promise you'll drop this if nothing works out?" I hold up my pinky.

Mila takes mine with hers and we shake. "Promise."

When Mila leaves, I finish my entries for the day in record time. I still technically have to work for another thirty minutes, so I stay logged in and grab my phone. Opening up DateMe, I check out Cole's profile again. Tall and skinny with more tattoos than I thought could fit on one arm.

Hey Cole! Would love to get together sometime!

There. Simple and to the point. After my epic failure of a date with Nash, I just want to be quick and concise. Hopefully, this will get Mila off my back. I open Candy Crush to pass the rest of the time, and soon a message rolls across my screen.

Would love to! Love the name by the way. Very edgy. Meet me tonight at The Big Oboe. 8:00. I'll wear a single red rose.

A sigh of ... relief? Frustration? I'm not sure. I know I told Mila I would try, but this doesn't even seem fun. This grumpy person is not me. I am holly jolly around this time of year. Stupid Nash ruined my holiday mood with his stupid face last night. Maybe Cole will be the perfect person to get me back in the spirit. I quickly Google The Big Oboe and find out it's a jazz club. I didn't even know jazz clubs were still around. I thought that kind of thing was only for people who were eligible for a senior citizen discount. You know what? It will be fine. No, it will be great.

When I notice the time, I log out and rush up to my closet. I have a cute blue-sparkle dress that would be perfect. When I can't find it, I do another search. Then look through my drawers.

"Mila!" I shout. When she doesn't answer, I shout again.

"What?" she asks through a yawn, coming into my room. She plops herself face down on my bed. I roll her over and she grunts in disapproval.

"Where is my blue dress? You know, the one with fringe and sparkles?"

Her eyes pop open and she laughs nervously. I know that laugh and narrow my eyes. She slowly climbs off my bed while holding her hands up in defeat.

"Mila," I speak calmly, "I thought we decided not to take clothes without asking each other."

Mila sidesteps until she's reached my door. "I didn't mean to ruin it."

She shrieks and runs down the hall with me quick at her heels. For someone who apparently is having the hangover from hell, she's pretty agile. Mila jumps over the ottoman, placing it between us as a barrier.

I laugh as I chase her. Torn between wanting to wring her neck and lock away my clothes so she can never find them. "I wanted to wear that tonight. What did you do with it?"

"Tonight? What's tonight?"

Mila fakes me out by pretending to go to her right and when I jump to attack, she sneaks around me.

"I'm sorry! I thought I told you about it. I'll buy you a new one!" she yells while running into the kitchen. Mila pulls the kitchen chairs in front of her and I hop from one to the other. When Trey appears in the hallway, Mila and I dart for him. Mila hides behind him, using him as her human shield while I try to reach for her. Trey holds up his hands. "What is happening?"

Mila and I are both breathing heavily as Trey makes us take steps away from each other.

"T, why are you chasing Mila?" Trey asks me as if he's now the mediator. I guess this has always been his role when Mila and I bicker over stupid things.

"Mila stole my dress and didn't ask permission."

"Mila, is that true?" Trey looks at her with disapproval. It's clearly fake, but I appreciate him trying.

"I meant to buy her a new one. I just completely forgot. It was the one I wore to Kyle's birthday ... when we were in the bathroom. Remember?"

Trey's eyebrows furrow together in question.

Mila sighs dramatically. "We were in the bathroom together when you said you didn't want to wait until we got home, but my dress got in the way—"

"Okay!" Trey claps his hands together loudly and I cover my mouth in horror.

Trey places the fakest smile on his face, "Tatum, Mila and I would like to apologize for misplacing your dress and would love to buy you another. Would that settle this matter?"

I nod while a smile takes over my features. Mila and I burst out laughing to the point where I fall on the floor and tears slip from my eyes.

"You know I hate when you borrow my clothes, but that's a pretty good excuse not to give it back," I joke and our laughter grows.

"I did ask," Mila explains. "You said I could take whatever."

"And what was I doing when you asked?" I giggle.

"I think watching TV."

"That explains it! I was in the zone and probably didn't even register you asked me a question."

"You two are so loud!" Trey complains while heading back to Mila's room.

After more apologies from Mila, she helps me pick out a chunky black sweater, dark jeans, and red-heeled boots. In addition to the mascara and eyeliner from this morning, I add some brown and black shadow to give my eyes a smoky look. I'm not sure what the kind of people who go to jazz clubs look like, but I think I look damn good. Mila, still feeling bad about my dress, lets me take her car again and I'm at The Big Oboe twenty minutes later.

A bouncer at the door asks for my ID and stamps my hand before allowing me inside. I'll admit, I do a little happy dance when he did that; I can't remember the last time I was carded. I walk through an almost pitch-black hallway which suddenly opens into what I only can assume is the perfect place for the mob. The entire club has a hushed feeling, with dark blue lights everywhere. Small booths are hidden in corners with only a few tables out in the open space. A stage holds a band playing some pretty amazing music and there's a small empty dance floor right in front of them. My eyes zero in on the bar hiding next to the stage. I keep my eyes peeled for a single red rose as I make my way through this weirdly quiet crowd. Everyone is just sitting and listening to the music, not talking or anything.

The bartender leans over the bar and cups his hand around his ear so he can hear me.

"Vodka and cranberry," I shout while taking a seat on the stool. My drink is delivered to me and I smile when it tastes better than the one from Sunny's.

"Tatum?"

I spin on my stool to find the tall, skinny guitarist from DateMe. Cole has the cutest bowtie I've ever seen and a single red rose is sitting in his fedora.

"Cole. I love the rose!" I'm forced to yell due to the music being so loud. He nods with a smile before ordering an Old-Fashioned.

"You look great," he says into my ear. "Have you ever been to a jazz club before?"

I shake my head.

"It's not as intimidating as it may seem. This is the type of club that focuses on the uniqueness of jazz music."

Keeping my smile in place takes effort because I think Cole just mansplained what a jazz club is. I said I had never been to a jazz club before, not that I didn't know what it was.

Cole grabs his drink and takes my hand. I follow him to a booth and slide in next to him. Taking another sip, I turn to him.

"How did you find out about this place?"

He shakes his head and places one finger to his lips indicating that I shouldn't be talking. Um, isn't that the entire point of a first date? Maybe he just wants me to wait until the end of this song. Giving him the benefit of the doubt, I take another sip of my drink and begin to tap my foot to the beat. The music is pretty good. I don't think I would listen to it regularly, but it goes with the vibe of this place.

Cole's hand finds my leg and I'm surprised at how forward he's being until I look over and see he's shaking his head. He's not trying to feel me up—he's telling me to stop tapping my foot. I sit frozen in place, feeling like a child who just got yelled at by her parents. Realizing it's been more than two minutes and the song still isn't over, I turn back to Cole.

"How long do they play for?"

Cole's mouth brushes my ear, "This isn't the kind of place where people talk. You come here to listen and absorb the music. Just sip your cocktail and feel the music. Quietly."

Wait, is he serious? "Then how are we supposed to get to know each other?"

No response. He just turns his attention back to the stage.

Taking a deep breath, I grab my phone out of my purse to check the time.

"You know, it's rude to be on your phone at a show. These musicians deserve your attention and respect. You should put it away," Cole orders.

Excuse him?

"I was just checking the time. I didn't know this was a show. I thought we would talk and get to know one another."

Nostrils flaring, he shakes his head. "The entire point of a jazz club is to listen to jazz music."

"Maybe I should go then," I say slowly.

No response.

Screw this. I don't need another asshole date. Grabbing my drink, I quickly stand up from the booth only to collide with a waiter. Unable to steady myself, I end up falling on my ass and hitting the back of my head on the table in the process. If that wasn't bad enough, I must've tightened the grasp on my glass, causing it to shatter in my hand. Red drops shine under the lights while Cole still stares at the stage. You have got to be kidding me.

The waiter crouches down next to me, "I am so sorry! Are you okay? Can I get you something?" When his eyes land on my right hand, he grabs a clean napkin from his apron. "Honey, you should go to the ER. That looks deep and I think there's some glass in there."

He wearily hands me the napkin while looking like he's trying not to throw up. Getting up and rushing out of this stupid club as fast as possible, I do notice that not a single person is looking at me. They're all absorbed in this stupid show. Gripping the napkins tighter, I do as the waiter said and go to the closest hospital. If anything, they can at least remove the shards of glass that are probably embedded in my hand now.

I'm at the hospital in under five minutes and give the nurse at the front desk my name, date of birth, and reason for being here. The annoying redhead pops her gum while typing my information into the computer. Dammit! I let another guy put me in a sour mood. How is this happening? I have never been like this. Normally I would say that going to that jazz club is a new experience. I would try and find the positive.

Stupid Nash. My bad mood started with him.

After being told to have a seat, I choose the chair closest to the Christmas tree decorated with white and blue ornaments. Maybe being in the tree's proximity will help my attitude.

A few minutes later, the redhead guides me back to Room Four and tells me the doctor will be in shortly. The smell of bleach invades my nostrils as I lie down on the bed. I asked the nurse earlier if I could at least get some gauze for my hand, which is now bleeding through the napkin, but she never answered me. I thought this was supposed to be an emergency room, where things happen quickly.

Another (nicer) nurse comes in and I give her more details about my head and hand. She is kind enough to exchange my bloody napkins with clean gauze. Once she leaves, I force myself to sit up. This mattress is doing nothing for my back. Facing away from the door, I look around the room. It looks like every single hospital room I've ever seen on TV.

"Good evening. I'm Dr. Anderson. What's going on?"

"No," I whisper to myself as I close my eyes. Seriously, can my night get worse?

Four

When I walked into the Emergency Department of St. Margaret's, it hadn't occurred to me who works here. As I slowly turn around, I'm met with the green piercing eyes that started all my grumpiness.

"Tatum?" Nash says with an equally surprised look. He looks like he's debating turning around to get another doctor when his eyes land on my bloody hand. "What happened?"

Rounding the bed, Nash pulls latex gloves over his impressively large hands and pulls away the gauze.

"Nothing. I mean a glass shattered in my hand. But I'm fine."

"Was that before or after you dumped its contents on someone?"

When I narrow my eyes, he apologizes. "Sorry, I'll continue to give you shit after we get this sewn up."

"You think it needs stitches?"

"Definitely. Just a few, though. It needs to be cleaned first, which I'll do after I perform your exam."

He pulls his bloody gloves off only to put another pair on. "I'm fine. I just need my hand fixed so I can go home and wash this horrible night off me."

Nash takes a step back, his eyes looking me up and down. "You seem different."

Rolling my eyes, I say, "There's no possible way you can determine that after only meeting me one time. Can you just get me another doctor?"

A low chuckle echoes through the room. "That's not how this works. Just shut up and let me do my exam." Nash's tone is teasing but I sit still, even when he shines his tiny little flashlight in my eyes.

"I said I'm fine—"

"Lay back," he says, his voice gentle but commanding. I do as he says.

"So you were just at a bar by yourself when you fell?" Nash questions as his fingers dance over my scalp.

"I didn't say I was at a bar."

Nash clears his throat, "I just assumed."

"Is that information pertinent?"

"It's just a question, Tatum."

Exhaling slowly, I decide to tell the embarrassing truth. "No. I was on a date."

"You waste no time."

I pull my head away, about to yell at him, when he laughs. "It was a joke. I'm sorry. Continue."

Nash resumes his examination as I do with my story. "I was getting up to leave and collided with a waiter. I hit the back of my head as I fell and I guess I clutched my glass too hard."

"This nurse said you came here alone," he says as if he's expecting me to tell him why.

"Do I need an escort to get proper medical care?"

Removing his gloves, he writes something on a notepad. "Once again, just a question."

I wonder if he needs to know this or if he's just a curious person by nature.

"Another dating app guy. He invited me to some jazz club, only to yell at me every time I talked. Apparently, it was some show. I pulled out my phone to check the time and he told me I was being rude. I tried to give him the benefit of the doubt and get to know him, but he blatantly ignored me. I was leaving when all this happened." I gesture to my head and hand, relieved to find Nash not smiling. He's not even snickering. He looks annoyed.

He disappears after ordering me to lie back on the bed and get comfy. I'm scrolling through pictures on my phone when the nice nurse appears, only to jab the biggest needle ever in my hand. Not long after that, my entire right hand is numb and I almost forget about the cut, the fall, the disastrous date. Man, if I never hear the words "jazz club" again, it will be too soon. I'm just about to beat level 164 in Candy Crush, which I've been stuck on for months, when Nash—I mean, Dr. Anderson—takes the phone from my good hand.

"Hey! Give that back!" I demand and he tosses it on the bed beside me.

"I just wanted to make sure you were prepared for what's about to happen next," he says in a formal tone.

"That would've been nice before I got stabbed in the hand with possibly the biggest needle in this hospital."

"It's not nearly the biggest, but if you want a tour I'm sure I could arrange one."

Nash sits on a stool next to my bed, placing my hand on a medical tray covered with what looks like a disposable absorbent pad.

"Can you feel this?" he asks while poking each of my fingertips with the tip of his pen.

I shake my head.

"How about this?" He runs his fingers over my palm, all while maintaining eye contact. It's weird how intimate this moment feels.

"No," I mumble while reminding myself to breathe.

Nash grabs a small needle before looking up at me through his eyelashes. "You might want to look away from this."

"You don't think I can handle it?"

Oh, my God. He was right. I should've looked away. I know my hand is completely numb, but watching a sharp piece of metal dig into your skin is not exactly something for the faint of heart. When he tugs on the thread pulling my skin together, I squeeze my eyes shut and swallow a very tiny amount of vomit. How the hell do people do this for a living? It's barbaric!

"And … done. You handled that like a champ," he praises and a small laugh escapes my lips. "I was kidding. You passed out before the first stitch."

I swear my head feels like it's getting heavier, but I shake the feeling off. "Well, there's nothing like watching someone repeatedly jam a piece of metal through your hand to wake you up."

Nash hands me a cup of water and orders me to drink. "The nurse is going to come in and finish bandaging your hand. She'll give you a list of instructions on how to take care of the stitches and I want to see you back in a week or so—"

"Why would I want to see you again?" Wow, okay that was not meant to sound so harsh.

Nash's eyebrows shoot up into his hairline. "I see I made an impression on you the other night. Look, I wanted to apologize—"

"No need." I hold my hand up to stop him and slide off the bed. "Everything is fine. I just really want to go home."

With a nod, Nash disappears. Okay, fine, I check out his butt as he walks away, but it's completely by accident.

When the nice nurse comes back, she informs me that the stitches in my hand will dissolve after a few days, so I just need to pay attention for signs of infection.

About forty-five minutes later, I park in my driveway, an instruction sheet in my good hand on how to take care of my bad hand. I lightly bang my head on the steering wheel a few times before getting out and heading inside.

The sound of chirping directly into my ear wakes me from the most perfect sleep and I groan in disapproval. I swing my hands in the air as if to hit the birds flying around my room only to realize it's my phone's ringtone. Grabbing it off the nightstand, I groan even louder when I see the name scrolling across the screen.

Mother—or, as I like to call her, Susan. That woman hasn't been a mother to me in ... well, it doesn't matter. It's only her first call this week, which is surprising. She couldn't bother being in my life when I was a teenager so I don't know why she calls so much now. It's not like I had a change of heart and suddenly forgive her for everything.

I don't even bother pressing ignore, I just let it ring until finally the call is sent to voicemail. Ha! Joke's on you. My voicemail has been full for weeks! It's probably petty of me that I don't listen to the voicemails she leaves me. I could delete them, but that's too much effort. I push myself to sit up and an overwhelming pain shoots through my hand. I forgot about my stitches. Why couldn't I have injured my left hand? I don't use it for anything!

Once the pain finally fades, I roll out of bed and grab the bottle of Advil I keep in my nightstand drawer. After I down three pills with some water, I get ready for the day while being very cautious not to re-injure my hand. I don't see or hear Mila, so I assume she went to work today. Oh, how I envy my best friend. Not only does she like her job, but she has goals. When we graduated college, she was determined to get a job in the restaurant industry. Her passion in life is to have her own bistro and she's well on her way to achieving that goal. Currently, she's the manager at Red House downtown. It's a cozy little speakeasy that is invitation only. Before she started working there, they were in danger of closing. Now, Red House is the number-one hidden gem of downtown Pittsburgh, thanks to Mila.

I start my workday with a call from my boss detailing the assignments that are high priority. These include if low-rise jeans are making a comeback, do people still wear actual animal fur, and how social media has shaped the new generation. I roll my eyes while using my perkiest voice to tell her I'll get it done. One thing I did not take into account is how difficult typing is now that I have a giant bandage on my hand. It's only Tuesday and this has already been the longest week of my life.

Five

"You staying in tonight?" Mila asks as I sit on the couch, shoveling popcorn into my mouth. She laughs when a few pieces miss my mouth and fall down the front of my shirt.

"Considering I already took my bra off for the day and am wearing a Rudolph onesie, the obvious answer would be yes. Why are you here? I assumed you'd be out with Trey."

Mila sticks her lower lip out before plopping down next to me. "His stupid friends wanted to play some stupid video games tonight."

I narrow my eyes in suspicion as my hand freezes halfway to my mouth, "Hmm. Interesting."

"What's interesting?"

"Usually you two are attached at the hip."

"Maybe I just missed you and wanted to hang out," she responds, shrugging her shoulders.

Nope. I'm not buying it. I cross my arms over my chest, purse my lips, and stare at her. She always folds after a few moments.

"Stop looking at me. I mean it, Tate!" Mila places her hand in front of her eyes, so she can't see me. I don't relent.

"Goddammit! Fine! I wanted to hang out with you, but I also wanted to know how the dating apps were going. This week was crazy and I barely saw you."

"I knew it!" I tease, grabbing the throw pillow behind my back and hitting her with it. "Well, it sucks to be you, because there's no news for me to tell you. Looks like you gave Trey a free pass for nothing."

Now it's Mila's turn to cross her arms. "I don't believe you for a second. What happened to the second guy? The one you were going to wear the blue dress for?"

"One, we don't speak of the blue dress. I'm still mourning it. Two, Cole was horrible. I swear the only men on these apps are ones who think women should sit there and be pretty. Oh, and show off her boobs."

"Cole asked to see your boobs?" Mila shrieks.

I shake my head, "No, but I keep getting messages from guys asking me to send them nudes. Seriously, are we like sixteen or something? Grow up."

"I'm sorry, Tater Tot. I promise not all men are creeps. You just have to find the right one. Did you ever message the other guys?" Mila grabs a handful of my popcorn.

"Beau and Brendon. They both were cute and seemed nice, but I thought the same thing about the previous two. Clearly, my radar is broken. Anyway, let's talk about something else."

"Fine. How's your hand feeling? You still never told me the name of your doctor."

She's fishing. Flustered from the events that took place that night, I ran into Mila when I got back from the ER. I knew she knew I was hiding something, but I said so few words and disappeared to my bedroom as quickly as possible.

"Why do you need to know my doctor's name?" I ask now.

A smile spreads across her lips. "Well, either you screwed your doctor or ran into someone you knew. Either way, spill."

Rolling my eyes, I sigh. "It was Nash."

"Nash? As in the first dating-app guy Nash?"

"Do either of us know another Nash?"

"Holy shit," she exhales. "Talk about fate."

My face puckers like I just sucked on a lemon. "Ew. No. He sewed up my hand in the most violent way possible and we barely talked. So, how are you and Trey doing?"

My distraction works because Mila perks up at the mention of his name. "We're great. I think he wants to take the next step."

"Which is … ?"

"We talked about living together. It wouldn't be immediate or anything, but we really love each other and just want to be together all the time."

My jaw drops open in shock. Living together? Wow, that's serious. Like, really serious. That would mean that eventually I would move out and be on my own. I've never lived on my own before. I went from college to living with Mila. As her best friend, I should be happy for her. Scratch that—I *am* happy for her. When I realize it's been at least thirty seconds and I haven't said anything, I clutch my hands over my heart and genuinely say, "That's adorable. See, that's what love should be. Where do you think you guys would live?"

"Not sure," she says, a little too fast. Mila grabs the remote from my good hand before she starts clicking buttons. "I know what will make you feel better."

The masterful creation that is the movie *Elf* starts playing on our television. We both chuckle as Mila grabs a blanket off the back of the couch to drape over us. Mila isn't as into Christmas as I am, but I know for a fact that *Elf* is her favorite movie. I bet she could probably put on a one-man show of it. The good friend in me should talk to Mila more about her relationship and how happy she is. However, the selfish friend in me seems to win out and I settle further into the couch.

When Buddy and Jovie go on their first date, I start to wonder if maybe Mila is right. Maybe I just haven't found the right guy. Obviously, I'm not going to find him while sitting on my couch watching Christmas movies. I pull out my phone and message Beau. He doesn't respond until I'm comfy in bed, but we make plans for tomorrow night. He even says he'll pick me up. Maybe my luck is about to change.

Saturday morning, the first day of December, Mila agrees it is now appropriate for the Christmas celebrations to begin. We need to start by hauling the Christmas tree bag out of my room and setting it up in the living room. Mila insists we make Trey do it. I refuse, and that's how I drop our Christmas tree on my baby toe. Mila's attempt to cover her laugh is pathetic and I look down to see if my new nickname will be Nine Toes Tatum.

"Want me to call up the hot doc to take care of you?" Mila teases.

"I told you. Nash and I barely spoke."

She nods while rolling her eyes.

Our fake tree is in two separate parts and as we're attempting to put it together, Trey shows up. Due to my injured hand, I need Mila's help with the bottom half, which is a lot easier with two people.

"I'm not taking anyone to the hospital," he says flatly.

Mila and I try to laugh, but the tree is surprisingly heavy and, as much as we don't want to admit it, we're struggling.

"You may need to," Mila pants. "Tatum already dropped the tree on her foot."

When we try, and fail, Mila pushes her lower lip out and softens her eyes, resulting in Trey narrowing his.

"No," he protests, "this is your thing. Aren't you two strong and independent women? Feminism and whatnot?"

"Oh, shut up and come help us."

Trey crosses his arms over his slender frame. "And what will I get for helping?"

A sigh of frustration bursts through my lips. "I will buy you your own stash of chocolate-drizzle cookies, but only if you hurry. This is really heavy!"

Without having to think twice, Trey steps in and saves us from any more potential medical emergencies.

Mila puts on a Christmas playlist, Trey makes us all some type of martini with crushed candy around the rim, and I lay out the ornaments on the couch. We spend the next hour adding lights, tinsel, ornaments, and a little bit of glitter to the tree. Due to our low ceilings, instead of an angel on the top of the tree, we add a gold glittery tiara. The next hour is spent with me decorating the house, Mila giving her opinion, and Trey napping. Realizing the time, I finish my drink and rush to get ready for my date.

I dress in a simple black dress that hangs off my shoulders and hugs my curves. I tug on some black stockings to help keep me from completely freezing outside. Mila insists on curling my hair and lets me borrow one of her sparkly clips to "complete the look," as she would say. I add my favorite Christmas tree earrings when she isn't looking.

Beau is exactly on time at seven thirty. Hugging my peacoat around me, Beau guides me to his 911 Turbo Porsche. I didn't know accountants made that much money. Maybe he works for Beyoncé?

"You look stunning," Beau says once we're both in the car. He places a gentle kiss on my hand before the engine roars to life. The car ride is pretty quiet while classical music flows through the speakers. I didn't know people listened to this kind of music unless they were in a concert hall or something.

"I'm really excited for dinner. Where are we going?" I ask and Beau smiles widely.

"It's a little restaurant I frequent from time to time. You'll love it. It has, hands down, the best food in town."

"That sounds delicious. So, can I ask why you're on a dating app?"

Beau chuckles low. "Right to the tough questions. I like that. Originally my friends set it up to mess with me, but I've met some great people through it."

"You've been online dating for a while?"

"Going on five months. Still waiting for the right one. I know she's out there."

That's ... optimistic.

Beau pulls up to the front of La Belle. The valet takes Beau's keys right before he jogs around the car to help me out. His hand a little too low on my back, Beau guides me through the revolving doors into probably the fanciest building I've ever seen: white marble floors, chandeliers hanging above us, and a floor-to-ceiling window running the entire length of the restaurant, overlooking downtown. We're seated right next to the window and I have the overwhelming feeling that tonight is going to be a good night.

"It's beautiful," I mutter as Beau pulls my chair out for me.

"And so are you," he whispers in my ear. My face heats up and I'm thankful for the dim lighting all around us. Within seconds our waiter appears with a wine menu.

"I'm not going to lie," I say. "I have no idea what I'm looking at. The way I pick out wines at the liquor store is by how pretty the label is."

I swear the waiter snickers in disapproval, but it's okay because Beau just laughs like it's a cute and funny quirk.

"We'll take the '96 Merlot. Thank you, Louis." Beau hands Louis the wine menu and with a nod, Louis disappears.

"I don't think I've ever been somewhere that has offered me three forks to eat with," I whisper, a little self-conscious.

"Don't be scared. Everyone has to start somewhere. I'll help you with the cutlery as the food comes out."

Beau's hand reaches across the table to grasp mine. I wince a little when he accidentally grazes my stitches. "What happened to your hand?"

"Oh. I'm just a klutz. Got cut by some glass the other day. No big deal."

We both smile and I release the tension I was holding in my shoulders. I run my hand through my curls while Beau's fingers rub over my knuckles.

"Are those Christmas trees?" he asks, squinting to look at my ears.

"Yeah! Christmas is my favorite time of the year. I have a pair of earrings for each day of the month."

Clearing his throat, he pulls his hand back and fans out his napkin before placing it in his lap. I take a sip of water while I wait for him to say something, ask another question, anything.

When a few moments of awkward silence pass, I ask, "Do you like Christmas?"

"God, no."

My jaw practically drops to the floor. Who doesn't like Christmas? I've heard of people like Beau, but didn't believe they existed.

"The noise and hustle and bustle of people who waited too long to shop—it's exhausting," he says. "And why should I spend my hard-earned money on people I only see a few times a year? It's not like they could afford to buy me anything useful. Not to mention this cold weather. It's horrific. Every year I say I'm going to move to the Caribbean, but my family is all here so I guess I'm stuck."

I smile awkwardly, wondering if this is some kind of joke. "Stuck? You're kidding, right?"

He shakes his head and takes a sip of his water. "Not at all. It would probably make my life if we could just skip over the entire season of winter."

OH. MY. GOD. Not liking Christmas is something that should have been in his profile. He could've written "I am extremely attractive, but I hate Christmas and wish the season would die in a fiery sleigh crash." I know this might sound crazy because I think I have chemistry with this guy, but I don't think I can be with someone who hates Christmas. I am happy little Cindy Lou Who, trying to get everyone in the holiday spirit and he is Ebenezer Scrooge who just kicked Tiny Tim's crutch out from under him.

The waiter presents our bottle of wine to Beau before pouring the smallest portion into each of our glasses.

"To new adventures," Beau announces, holding his glass in the air and waiting for me.

I open my mouth to speak but have no idea what I want to say. Am I going to risk finding a happy ever after because of some little hiccup like hating Christmas?

"I have to go," I say before standing up.

"Wait, what?" Beau is up and at my side in an instant. "You have to go? Is everything okay? I thought the date was going great."

"You hate Christmas."

"So? I didn't say I hate you." There's a slight edge to his tone.

"Christmas is my thing. It's my favorite time of the year and this year I've been struggling to keep my spirits up. I'm sorry. You seem very nice, but I just don't think this is going to work out."

Beau tilts his head to the side, running a hand over his small amount of stubble.

"I can't believe this. You're serious?"

"Beau, I'm so—"

"Have fun finding a ride home."

Beau, not looking at me, grabs my glass of wine, downs it in one gulp then grabs his. "You can leave now." He actually makes a shooing motion with his hand. My mouth drops open in horror, but then I remember, I was the one who wanted to leave. Ignoring his pettiness, I head to the door while digging for my phone in my purse. I pull up my Uber app only to find out that the next car can be here in thirty-five minutes.

"Thirty-five minutes?" I say out loud. Normally that wouldn't be bad, but I have no idea where I am and it's freezing outside. My stockings, while cute, do nothing to keep me warm.

I walk over to the valet. "Excuse me. I can't get a car for a while. Is there a bar or somewhere I can wait?"

"Steve's Joint is down the road. Just be careful walking there. That part of the road is brick." I thank him and head in the direction he pointed. When the wind picks up, I walk faster, trying to shield my face with my hands. To my disbelief, the night grows much worse when I slip on a patch of ice and scrape my knee.

A sigh of relief washes over me when I spot the giant red letters in the distance. A gust of wind practically pushes me through the door, causing me to stumble like an idiot. The scent of liquor invades my nostrils as I sweep my hair out of my face and make my way to the bar. Steve's Joint is a small tavern with only a few tabletops and a long bar along the wall. The atmosphere seems quiet and relaxed, like a place where you can hear the person next to you talk while enjoying your favorite drink. Luckily it's not too crowded and I find an empty stool. As soft rock echoes from the jukebox hiding in the corner, I glance up at the chalkboard menu on the wall.

"What'll you have?" a man who is more beard than skin asks me.

Sliding out of my jacket, I sit and place it over my lap. "Hm, do you have any holiday specials?"

One eyebrow quirks up. "Lady, does this look like a place that has holiday specials?"

Looking around the room, I shrug. "Would you be willing to make something Christmassy?"

He rubs a hand over his face. "I don't know what that means."

"Like something red or green, or with peppermint. Oh, maybe you could use a candy cane as a garnish?" I'm grasping at straws here. The bartender probably thinks I'm a loon.

He leans closer to me and lowers his voice. "I don't mean to be rude, but are you serious right now?"

My holiday mood starts to deflate. Again. I thought after watching Christmas movies and dancing in my PJs to holiday classics that it was back, but I must've been wrong. Is it weird that I love Christmas? I feel like the nerdy girl in school who has no friends with the way the bartender is looking at me right now.

My spirit collapses as I mumble, "I'll just take a vodka and cranberry, please."

Six

- -

"Holy hell, are you following me?"

My eyes widen at the husky voice, and I look at the man sitting three barstools away. Nash's eyes seem brighter than the last time I saw him, and his hair looks like he styled it to appear like he just rolled out of bed. His grip on his tumbler tightens, forcing my eyes to his biceps. Has he been working out? Damn him for looking so good.

"Am I following you? Are you insinuating that I hit my head and cut my hand just so I could come visit you? That I willingly let you penetrate my skin with a needle for the hell of it?"

A smile spreads across Nash's face and I notice the tiniest dimple in his left cheek. "I don't think that's an appropriate usage of the word 'penetrate.'"

"Oh my God, how old are you?" I huff.

He laughs. "I'm here because I met a friend from work who lives right around the corner. He actually just left and I stayed because I wanted to finish my drink." Nash slides down to the stool next to me. "What happened to your knee?"

I slide my lower half away from him. "Nothing."

He takes a sip of his drink, running his tongue over his lower lip. "How's the hand?"

My eyes travel to the white gauze wrapped around my stitches. "Sore, but alcohol helps."

"You never told me what you're doing here."

Man, I wish I had that drink right about now. Tapping my foot anxiously against the barstool, I whisper, "I don't want to tell you."

"And why not?" he asks, sipping the brown liquor.

I exhale sharply. "Because I was on another horrible date, okay?"

Nash bumps his shoulder to mine. "At least you didn't end up in the emergency room this time."

I look over at him, wanting to yell and scream, but instead, I start to laugh. Like full-blown obnoxious laughing at how ridiculous and awful this night has been.

"For the lady." The bartender sets my drink down in front of me with a candy cane garnish.

I can't help my wide smile. "I knew you could make a Christmas-themed drink. Thank you!"

I swear his cheeks flush a little when I grab the candy cane and begin to suck on the end.

"See?" Nash points to my drink. "Things are looking up."

A ping alert has me checking my phone. "Spoke too soon. My Uber just canceled. Can they even do that?"

"Apparently they can, but only to you," he jokes.

I roll my eyes, but it only makes him laugh more.

"If it makes you feel better, I haven't had much luck in the dating pool either."

"Why? You're such a catch," I deadpan, stirring my drink with my half-eaten candy cane. A smirk crosses his face like he's trying not to laugh. "Are you trying to make a joke?"

I turn my entire body towards him. "I think our dates are going badly for completely different reasons. I doubt the majority of your messages are unwanted genital pictures."

"And what makes you think that?"

A laugh bubbles in my throat. Sitting this close to Nash, in a rather pleasant mood, I notice the smallest features about him. His right ear sits just slightly lower than the other even though he has excellent posture. A small scar above his left eyebrow that can only be seen when he creases his forehead. It's not fair that someone this good-looking has such an annoying personality.

"So, are you going to let me look at your knee or what?"

I take a sip of my drink. "I didn't know you were on call. Am I using that terminology right?"

Nash chuckles before waving at the bartender. "I need a Band-Aid and some gauze."

"Is this covered by my insurance?" I ask.

His slow blink tells me he's not amused.

Nash grabs my stool, twisting it so my body is facing his, and nods to my knee. "May I?"

"Why the hell not?" I say, taking another drink.

Using the gauze, he gently dabs my knee.

"You know these stockings are trashed, right?" Just as I'm about to answer, he tears an even larger hole in them.

"What is wrong with you?!" I shriek.

Nash unwraps the Band-Aid and places it over my cut. "Band-Aids don't stick to stockings."

His left hand wraps around the back of my leg to steady me and my breath turns shaky. He feels warm and nice. As his fingers gently press the Band-Aid on my knee, I whisper, "You're good at that."

Instantly regretting my words, I cover my mouth. What did the bartender put in my drink?

Nash's eyebrow quirks up, "Good at what?"

Our eyes meet and for a brief second, I notice a bluish tint to the green. "At, um, taking care of people. Taking care of me."

"That sounds like a compliment."

I bring my cup to my lips, trying to hide my smile.

"What made you want to become a doctor?" I ask.

Nash takes a slow drink from his glass and I struggle to keep my eyes off his lips. "Like you said, I'm good at taking care of people."

We both laugh. "You know, you are great at fitting the cocky doctor stereotype."

He shakes his head. "Not cocky. Confident. You have to be in my line of work."

"Seems like a very fine line," I tease.

Nash's smile is genuine and pretty adorable. "Let's not talk about me. Didn't you say you're a writer?"

My eyebrows shoot up in surprise. "Yes, I did. I can't believe you remembered."

"Believe it or not, I listened to everything you said. I was really excited to go out with you."

Heat creeps up my neck and I have to remind myself to breathe. "Come on, tell me. What kind of writer?"

I open my mouth, not sure if I should say. Not that many people know I've written a book. In all honesty, I don't tell people because I'm nervous nothing will ever come of it. And if I keep it a secret, then I don't look like such a failure. Then again, I most likely will never see Nash again, so what's the harm?

"I wrote a novel," I say slowly, nervous about his reaction.

His eyes widen. "Holy shit! Like a novel novel?"

I giggle. "What other kind of novel would I write?"

He shrugs. "I don't know. I've never met a person who wrote a book. Is it published? Can I buy it somewhere?"

I open my mouth to respond, but only squeaks come out. I think I'm in shock because I didn't expect that response. Maybe a quip about how becoming an author is a pipe dream, but not genuine interest in my writing. "N-no, it's still a work in progress."

"Well, let me know when it's in stores. I'd like to read it."

I cock my head to the side. "You don't even know what it's about."

"Call it a hunch, but I feel that you can probably create some awesome stories."

Nash and I are getting along surprisingly well that I don't register we're already on our second drink of the night. I'm starting to feel more relaxed and can't exactly remember what I disliked about him.

Yes, he was kind of a jerk on our date, but he also is the guy who sewed up my hand and bandaged me up. He can't be all that bad. Plus, it wouldn't be fair to the women of the world for a man who looks like him to be a total and complete ass.

"So why do you do it?" I ask while watching the condensation drip down onto the wooden bar.

"Do what?" Nash chuckles.

"The dating app. You're hot. I find it hard to believe you can't find someone to screw during your shifts."

He chokes on his drink and I giggle as I tap his back. "I might not have gone to medical school, but I am CPR certified."

Nash clears his throat. "I did not expect that from you, sweetheart."

I roll my eyes and finish the liquid in my glass. "Benny! Can I get another Tatum's Candy Cane, please?"

Yes, I have made friends with the bartender and yes, he has named my drink after me. I have to say the drinks are on the weaker side, but just the fact that I have my own special drink puts me in a good mood.

"Sure thing. Give me a second," he hollers.

"You know that title makes you sound like a stripper," Nash mumbles.

"Whatever. You're just jealous that Benny didn't name a drink after you."

Nash pokes me in the ribs. "You admitted I was hot."

Tilting my head to the side, I tap my chin. "Nope. I don't think I did. Why would I lie to you like that?"

"Haha. You think I'm hot."

"No, I don't," I whine while nudging his shoulder with mine.

"If you admit that you think I'm hot, I'll tell you what I think about you."

"That's something I probably don't want to know."

Nash licks his lips before invading my personal space. "I'd tell you that I think you are the most stubborn, annoying, beautiful woman I've ever seen in my life and I would like nothing more than to take you back to my place. I'd also tell you that ever since you dumped your drink in my lap, I haven't been able to stop thinking about you."

My breath catches in my throat. Am I drunk? Nash's dimple is back and I swear his eyes just traveled down to my lips. I lick them instinctively and now I know for sure he's watching them. A quick glance at Nash's straining zipper tells me that he's as turned on as I am. My hand falls on Nash's knee and I lean in towards him.

"One Tatum's Candy Cane," Benny announces, causing me to jump in surprise and almost fall off my chair. Nash grabs my elbow to steady me and I thank him. I bring the glass tumbler to my lips as heat rushes to my cheeks. What is happening? I'm not supposed to find Nash charming. He's arrogant and rude and an all-around jerk. Right?

Nash rubs a hand over his five o'clock shadow. "I'm on the app because dating is hard, and finding someone I'm willing to date is even harder."

"But don't you just meet a lot of weirdos? I mean, I think I've lost count of the number of messages I got asking me to send pictures of my chest."

Nash chokes on his drink, bringing a shy smile to my face. "Well, as I am a man without a wonderful rack, I do not have that problem."

I tilt my head to the side. "Careful, Nash. You keep giving me compliments and I'm going to think you like me."

"Who says I don't?"

Is it possible for all the air to suddenly be sucked out of the room? That must be what's happening since I'm having trouble breathing. As Nash's lips part, I wonder what they would taste like. Maybe a hint of smokiness from the booze? Is he a slow and sensual kisser or the kind who would want to bite and seduce your mouth like it's his dying wish? Just when I finally catch my breath, Nash tucks a rogue strand of hair behind my ear. Both of us are completely aware of the fact that his hand lingers on my neck.

"Those are some pretty festive earrings."

Moment ruined. Sighing, I turn back to my drink. "I get it, okay? They're dorky. But it's Christmas and I like them, so why does everyone—"

"Whoa." Nash holds his hands up in defense. "I wasn't making fun of you. I was just stating a fact. I like them. They're cute."

My shoulders slump. "Oh. Sorry. The guy from tonight basically made fun of my earrings and told me he hates Christmas, so I guess I'm a little sensitive."

His brows pinch together in confusion. "How can anybody hate Christmas? That's like hating Betty White and no one hates Betty White."

We both chuckle and it feels comfortable. Maybe too comfortable. Sitting this close makes me notice the little crinkles around his eyes when he smiles. As sweet as he's being now, I can't forget about how he acted on our date. Getting involved with him would probably be a horrible mistake.

I finish the rest of my drink, underestimating how much is still in the glass. "I think I should go."

"Go? Already?" When I turn to meet Nash, he looks ... upset. Disappointed, almost. My fingers clutch around my wallet but I can't seem to pull it out of my purse. I guess another drink wouldn't kill me.

"Maybe just one more?" I mumble and Nash's smile spreads to his eyes. Since I met him, I don't think I've seen him this happy.

Nash orders us each a water and while I wait, I steal his drink. It's smooth and smoky going down. I'm shocked because I didn't think I liked Scotch. When Benny brings my drink, I gladly surrender Nash's.

"Don't you have a tattoo?" I ask.

Nash's eyes are glued to my mouth as I lick my lips.

When I nudge his leg, he clears his throat. "What did you say?"

I giggle. "I asked if you had a tattoo."

"Want to see it?" he asks with the evilest expression.

Pulling my lower lip between my teeth, I nod my head. Nash rolls up the sleeve of his shirt, revealing a compass on his elbow with intricate line work flowing through it. Without thinking, I reach forward and run my fingertips over the artwork. He probably thinks I missed it, but his sharp intake of breath when my fingers touch his skin sends a bolt of heat between my legs.

"It's beautiful."

"Yeah, it is," he says and when I look up, he's staring at me.

"So, I had a thought," Nash starts, pausing for dramatic effect.

Pulling my hand back, I gesture for him to continue as I take a drink.

"We should have sex."

I'm forced to cover my mouth so I don't spit water across the room. What did he just say? Am I going deaf? There's no way I heard him correctly.

"I'm sorry, I didn't realize sex with me was so repulsive."

I look around before lowering my voice. "Why on Earth would I have sex with you? We don't even like each other."

"Coming from the woman who has been staring at my lips half the night and my crotch the other half. Be honest: how many times have you thought about kissing me tonight?"

Crap! How does he know?

"That's not the point," I stutter and shake my head.

"I'm not asking you to marry me. We're adults and can make mature decisions. Besides, it was just a thought. Like a friends-with-benefits kind of thing." Nash brings his tumbler to his lips, pausing briefly before taking a drink.

"Friends with benefits without the friends part?" I don't mean to sound like a total asshole, but it's an honest question.

Nash chuckles. "Sure." His eyes scan down my body and my pulse quickens. Maybe sex with Nash wouldn't be a bad thing. For one, he's insanely hot. Plus, it's been quite a while since I've done the horizontal mambo. Now that I think about it, maybe I'm single because I say stuff like "horizontal mambo." Note to self: Never, ever, say that phrase in front of Nash.

I open my mouth to give him my answer when he slams his lips against mine. A small gasp escapes me and he uses the opportunity to sweep his tongue across mine. Nash tangles his fingers in my hair as I grip onto his shirt for dear life. He slides off his bar stool, closing the distance between us. Is this what every kiss is supposed to feel like? The all-consuming wanting to jump in the air and fist pump because it's the most amazing sensation you've ever experienced? I've been kissed before, but never like this.

When Nash pulls away, I unconsciously whimper at the loss of contact.

"Want to come back to my place?" he pants while still holding me in place by my hair. Unable to form any coherent thoughts, I just nod my head and smile.

Then I pull my hand away from his chest. "I just, um, need to use the restroom first."

Nash takes my hand, helping me off the stool. I feel his eyes on my backside the entire way to the bathroom and it brings a smile to my lips. My God, I'm acting like a preteen who just had her first kiss. The bathroom has a single stall, a sink, and a mirror. After I make sure the door is locked, I confront my reflection.

"You need this. Sex is a good thing. You can do this. Sex doesn't involve talking—well, sort of. I mean, if Nash is talking during sex ... Oh, my God. I wonder if Nash is a dirty talker." I shake my head. "Back to the point." I press my finger to my chest and then aim it at my reflection. "You are a goddess and you deserve to be treated like one. Make sure Nash does or kick his ass to the curb. For a second time."

Feeling confident, triumphant, and a little tipsy, I flip my hair behind my shoulder before blowing a kiss to the mirror.

I pull open the door and am greeted by a tall, skinny blond clapping her hands together with a tear rolling down her cheek. "That was beautiful, girl. You are a goddess! Now go show Nash what he's missing!"

"Ready?" Nash asks when I make my way back to the bar.

"Yeah, let me just pay my tab." I lean forward to try to get Benny's attention, but Nash wraps his fingers around my elbow and guides me away.

"It's taken care of."

Jerking my elbow out of his hand, I turn to face him. "Why did you do that? I am perfectly capable of paying for my drinks."

Instead of sighing and stomping away like I expect him to do, he smiles and chuckles. "I know you are, sweetheart. Just think of this as my making up for not paying for your awful drink at Sunny's."

"You mean the one I dumped all over your crotch?" I giggle at the memory.

"Why are you thinking about my crotch? Is there something you want to tell me?" Nash teases and I roll my eyes.

Nash holds the door for me and helps me climb into the silver Honda waiting for us outside before he enters behind me. We stay on our respective sides of the car the entire way to his house while our hands gently rest on the seat separating us. I wonder what would happen if I reached over. Would he hold my hand? Or maybe he would pretend he had an itch or something to avoid the whole interaction. Don't get me wrong: I don't want to hold his hand because I want to be his girlfriend or anything, but since that kiss, I feel like everything has changed. I just want his rock-hard chest pressed against mine while his long fingers travel down my sides. His lips owning every inch of my skin while I gasp in excitement—

"Tatum?"

"Mhmm?" Oh God, he can't read minds. Can he?

"I'm really glad I ran into you tonight."

Seven

After texting Mila that I would be home late, the car pulls over into a loading zone while we get out. Nash grabs my hand to help me but releases it the second the car speeds away. With his hand on my lower back, and I mean lower back, he guides me into the tallest brick building I've ever seen, nodding at the doorman.

"Evening, Jeeves."

"Mr. Anderson," Jeeves says as he tips his hat.

"Jeeves?" I whisper once we're far enough away, snuggling into Nash. "There's no way that's his real name. He totally changed it just for this job."

Nash laughs at me as he presses the button for the elevator. His hand is still on my back and I am forced to focus on my breathing, not the feeling in the pit of my stomach. In and out. In and out. When we walk into the elevator, Nash takes something out of his wallet and swipes it in front of a scanner above the buttons.

"What the hell is that? Crap! Are you some type of serial killer taking me to your secret lair because I pissed you off with the whole drink-in-the-lap thing?"

It's a joke ... sort of.

Looking at me with hooded eyes, Nash leans down and whispers in my ear, "I assure you that I'm not a serial killer. But I will make you pay for the drink. You ruined my favorite pants."

A lump blocks my airway and I have to remember how to swallow. Is it bad that part of me hopes he's being serious?

When the chrome doors open, I'm momentarily blinded by the insanely white room we step into. Nash places his keys, wallet, and phone in a bowl on the shelf next to us while I stand with my jaw permanently on the floor. White marble covers pretty much every inch of his PENTHOUSE! Yes, I said penthouse! I slip out of my heels and walk through the entryway.

"Want something to drink?" he asks while heading to the kitchen. White and gray quartz counters with top-of-the-line appliances and the most pristine white cabinets I have ever seen in my life. How do you even keep something that white?

"Water would be great," I mumble as I continue my self-guided tour.

Beautiful black leather sofas sit on top of a cream-colored shag rug in the living room. A thin Christmas tree with white lights and simple black and red ornaments makes the room feel cozy. I think my heart stops when I see what has to be at least a seventy-inch TV hanging on the wall above a fireplace that has a few picture frames on the mantel. I step closer to look at the pictures and smile. One where he's in a white lab coat with a stethoscope around his neck and a graduation cap on his styled head of hair. One where his arm is around a blond girl who is crossing her eyes and sticking out her tongue while he makes an equally silly face. The final one is of him smiling while holding a furry black and white ball. I forgot he had a cat! I look around again and frown. How the hell does he have a cat in this pristine penthouse? It seems entirely impossible.

"Where are your other decorations? I thought you said you liked Christmas."

Nash's chuckle echoes through the open space. "I have a Christmas tree. I know this will surprise you, but I'm not much of a decorator."

"Well, that's not acceptable. We'll have to change that."

"Here you go," Nash appears next to me, handing me a glass filled with ice water. I thank him and take a sip, unable to look away from him.

Shifting my weight from one foot to the other, I give a weak smile. So, we're here. In his house. All alone. To do something in our silence, I chug most of the water in my glass.

"You have a cat," I say and he laughs.

"Yeah. Smelly Cat's at her aunt's tonight."

"You have a sister?" I ask, genuinely interested.

He nods and gestures to the picture frames, "The blond one who looks like a psycho. She was the one who helped me rescue Smelly Cat and guilts me into sharing her."

"I like cats. I had a tiny little orange one growing up, but she ran away when I was six."

His brow furrows, "That's awful. I'm sorry."

"I'd love to meet Smelly Cat."

He smiles. "Maybe one day."

Wait, we're not supposed to be talking. We're supposed to be having sex. How did I already reveal something personal about myself? This isn't supposed to be about getting to know each other. It's supposed to be about getting naked, getting laid, and then getting the hell out of Dodge.

"Have you ever done the friends-with-benefits kind of thing?" I ask, placing my drink down on a coaster.

He shakes his head, one hand in his pocket while the other holds his glass.

"Me neither," I say while sliding down the zipper at my side.

His eyes widen and I silently laugh. Biting my lip to appear sexy, I slide the sleeves off my shoulders and wait for the dress to pool at my feet. It doesn't do that. Frowning in confusion and wanting to maintain the sexy vibe, I wiggle my hips to try to get the fabric to move. Nash's eyebrows raise in question. I force a smile and try to pull on the fabric. Nothing. What the hell? It takes me a moment to realize this dress only likes to come off one way, over my head. While that isn't overly attractive, I choose to go with it.

"Everything okay?" he asks with a hint of laughter in his tone.

"Great." I look him up and down as my tongue darts out of my mouth. "Bedroom?"

He points to a door hidden in the shadows. Walking in front of him so he can't see me wrestling with this stupid dress, I grab the hem and start to lift it over my head, careful of my bandaged hand. When I'm mostly free of the tight material, it somehow gets caught on my favorite earrings. This results in the fabric being stuck over my eyes and me running face-first into what I can only assume is the door frame. I fall back into something hard and when Nash helps me rip the dress off, I realize it was his chest. I wish I could blame the clumsiness on my being drunk, but I'm barely buzzed anymore. I start laughing like a hyena and laugh even harder when Nash joins me.

Nash's strong hands cup my face when both of us calm down. His thumb rubs over my cheekbone and eager-beaver me jumps up on my tiptoes to kiss him. Something in the universe must be off because instead of our lips connecting for another mind-blowing kiss, our foreheads collide with a loud THUNK.

"Ouch!" I whine while he grabs his head. "I don't think this is working."

"No, it's working. Kind of," he mutters unconvincingly.

"So far, I got stuck in my dress and hit myself in the head twice. Do you have any Advil?"

He nods while I sit down on the couch. A shiver runs up my spine as the cold leather meets my bare back.

"Here." He sets two orange tablets in my hand and hands me my water cup.

"Thanks." I down the pills and slump back on the cushions. My eyes dart around the room for a blanket. I'm cold, but not cold enough to put that stupid dress back on.

When Nash disappears, I lean my head back and shut my eyes. Maybe the ground can just open and swallow me whole right now. That wouldn't be the worst thing.

My eyes pop back open when I feel something fall into my lap. When I look at Nash with a questioning glance, he just smiles.

"You look cold and we can't take another chance with that dress. Bathroom's right behind you."

Grabbing the black fabric, I scurry through the door he directed me to. I don't know why I'm surprised, but I'm pretty sure the bathroom is bigger than my bedroom. Jacuzzi tub, glass shower, and double vanity. I would be completely content to move into this bathroom.

I quickly shimmy out of my ruined stockings and tug on the black sweatshirt and joggers he gave me. They are surprisingly comfortable. So comfortable that I don't think I'm ever going to give them back. When I emerge from the bathroom, there's a fire going in the fireplace, the TV is turned on, and Nash is sitting on the couch, channel surfing, with a plush gray blanket across his lap. He pats the seat next to him and I join him, cuddling under the blanket. As I try to get comfortable, Nash sighs. He pushes my shoulders back, causing me to lie back and rest my head on a throw pillow while he grabs my feet and places them across his lap.

He gasps. "Your feet are little icicles!"

"That's what happens when you're stupid enough to wear stockings in the middle of winter."

"You're far from stupid," he says as he wraps the blanket around my feet. "How's the knee feeling?"

"Better. Thanks to Dr. Anderson." I smile.

Nash laughs at my comment. "Anything you want to watch?"

I pull the hood up over my hair. "I thought we were supposed to be having sex. Isn't that what friends with benefits is? Where's my sex?"

Nash chuckles, "Well, considering the number of injuries you've already received, I'm thinking tonight might not be our night."

"I should go home," I mumble half-heartedly, making a move to sit up.

"It's really that awful spending time with me?" His voice is quiet as he finally moves his attention from the TV to me.

"No," I answer honestly. "I just figured you would want me gone after we, well, you know."

Nash wraps his hands around my feet. "I don't want you to leave, but if you want to go, I can call you a car."

After a moment, I shake my head. "I don't want to leave."

Resting my head on the pillow, Nash puts on *Santa Claus Is Coming to Town* and begins to rub my feet. "Are you starting to warm up?"

I nod my head and pull the blanket up to my chin. "This is one of my favorite Christmas movies."

"Mine too."

I'm a little surprised at the intimate gesture. I've never had a guy rub my feet before. A quiet moan escapes me when his thumb presses the right spot. Unintentionally, my eyes flutter shut, and my back arches off the couch. Holy crap, is he trying to give me an orgasm this way? Because I wholeheartedly believe that he could. My eyes wander quickly over to Nash and I smile when I find him looking back at me. He pushes the tender spot again and we both chuckle when I gasp. This is not at all what I expected when I agreed to go home with him. I don't doubt sex with Nash is great, but this is pretty amazing all on its own.

"I don't mean to be rude, but can I ask you something?"

Nash nods and licks his lips. Does he not realize how distracting that is?

"I know doctors make a lot of money, but this is a penthouse. Like, celebrities live in penthouses."

He laughs as he scrubs his hand down his face. "That's not a question. But yes. I make good money as a doctor, but I come from old money. My great-grandfather was a bigwig who knew how to invest. Believe it or not, this penthouse was on the cheaper side of the houses I was looking at."

My mouth falls open. "Cheaper side? Were you trying to buy a town or something?"

Nash continues to laugh at my absurdity and it's a mesmerizing sound. I could listen to that laugh all day.

"Tell me about yourself," Nash says when we're halfway through the movie. He's stopped rubbing my feet but is still holding on.

I nudge him. "Shh, you're missing the movie."

"I'm serious. What about your family? Any holiday plans with them?"

My pulse spikes at his question and I focus on the movie when I say, "Pass."

"What? You can't pass on a question."

"I just did," I say, pulling my feet out of his grasp and tucking them under my body.

Nash exhales sharply. "All right. What about your job? You said you've been busy lately. What have you been writing?"

"Pass."

Nash runs his hands through his hair in frustration. "You can't pass on every question. Do you not know how to have a regular conversation?"

I thought this was supposed to be just a sex thing. Why is he asking such invasive questions?

"Oh, I'm sorry if I don't want to answer those very specific questions. Why don't you ask me something more normal? Like my favorite ice cream flavor or favorite color? Why would I want to get into heavy shit when I don't even know you?"

A wave of heat takes over me and I toss the blanket off my lap. Nash's hands slap his thighs before he stands up. "Seriously? You don't want to talk so you're threatening to leave again? My God, are you not capable of having a normal conversation unless booze is involved?"

"Screw you!" I shout and stand up. "I was hot and was just taking the blanket off, but since I don't know how to live up to your ridiculous standards, I'll just leave!"

I go to stomp past Nash when he grabs my elbow and stops me.

"And I'm taking the comfy sweats with—" I shout before Nash's lips crash on mine. His lips are soft and at the first feel of his tongue sweeping across my lower lip, I open my mouth for him. He cups my face and pulls me closer, deepening the kiss. My hands find his waist, grabbing and twisting the fabric of his shirt. I moan into his mouth when his fingers tangle in my hair and tug. I pull him closer to me as his tongue explores every inch of my mouth. If I thought the kiss at the bar was amazing, I don't even have words to describe this one. Nash's hands disappear for a brief moment before he hooks them under my thighs and lifts me. I wrap my legs around his waist as we move. I have no idea what is happening and I don't even care. Feeling him grow underneath me, I pull myself closer and smile when a low growl comes from Nash. Our lips leave each other's only long enough for me to tear the sweatshirt off. When I toss it across the room, I hear something crash. Nash doesn't seem to care as he lays me down on his bed.

Or on a cloud. I don't think I can tell the difference.

I bring my lower lip between my teeth as he scales my body with dark eyes. Not looking away, I slide backward until I meet the headboard. Nash's breaths are shallow as he climbs on the bed, stalking me. When I lean up to kiss him, he chuckles before burying his head in my neck. His lips and teeth bite and tease me all while I'm silently praying he never stops. As he continues his assault on my skin, my fingers fumble to unbutton his shirt and then slide it off his incredibly toned body.

"Birth control?" he asks between pants.

"What?"

"Are you on birth control?"

"Has anyone ever told you that your idea of dirty talk is incredible?"

He chuckles and I feel the vibration against my hands. "I'm just asking because—"

"I know why you're asking. I'm just giving you a hard time. And yes, I am on birth control. I'm clean, too."

Wrapping my arms around his neck, I force us to roll over.

"Me too."

Straddling and looking down at him, my lips part in awe.

"How does an emergency room doctor who works double shifts have the time to get these?" I ask as I trail my finger down his six-pack. This man has muscles in places I didn't even realize it was possible to have muscles. Nash pushes himself up, grabbing the back of my neck and meeting my lips once again. This kiss is gentle and loving. At least, it was before he bit my lower lip.

"You like that?"

I nod, panting hard. "I like it rough."

Somehow my bra falls to the ground (when did he even undo the clasp?) and his head dips to my chest.

"I can do rough."

I swear my eyes roll to the back of my head when he nips and teases me in the best ways. His teeth sink into my skin and I arch my back.

He looks up, finding my eyes. "Too much?"

I shake my head. "More. Please, more."

He rolls me to my back. My breath catches in my throat as his hand skims down my stomach, over the fabric of my panties. His fingers tease me through the material and I move my hips, trying to get what I want.

He arches a brow. "And I thought you didn't like me."

"Nash," I moan.

His pants are gone before I can even blink and I lift my hips to help him remove my last article of clothing.

"You are a goddess," he mumbles into my skin before licking a trail of kisses up my calf, knee, and thigh. An unintelligible noise flies from my mouth when his tongue reaches his destination. My fingers twist into the sheets and my legs start trembling. Can one see stars from a guy doing this? Because I swear I can see every constellation in the sky right now.

"Still want to leave?"

"Why'd you stop? Nash, please—"

One long, agonizingly slow drag of his tongue has me forgetting my next words. My legs tighten around him as he continues to lick and swirl every inch of me. My teeth clamp down on my lower lip when two fingers are pushed inside me. The combination of his tongue, lips, and fingers have me struggling to remember my name. My toes curl and Nash's name leaves my lips in a long, slow moan as the pressure inside me continues to grow and grow until I explode in one of the most epic orgasms of my life—and no, I'm not exaggerating. A smile spreads across my face as I pant for dear life.

"Well, that was good for me. I'm going to go now," I tease.

With an evil grin, Nash leans down and kisses me. Hard. Rough. My fingers twist into his hair and tug when I feel him enter me. Our breaths are ragged as we get used to the feel of each other.

"Tatum, holy hell!"

His movements start slow like he's trying to savor every moment. Nash's hand finds my breast, squeezing and kneading as his hips move faster. My legs wrap around his waist as we move together. Completely in sync.

When I met Nash, I never would've thought there would be something we would be able to do together.

Oh, how I was so incredibly wrong.

"Faster," I pant.

He increases his speed with a cocky grin and slams into me, hitting that perfect spot. Over and over. I can't believe I was ever contemplating saying no to sex with Nash. He starts to do this circle thing with his hips while he continues his thrusts and I fall apart in seconds. A drop of sweat drips down Nash's chest and I want to lick it off.

"Don't stop," I plead. "Never stop."

Nash's hand slides down my body, his fingers finding the small bundle of nerves between my legs. My nails dig into his shoulders as I tighten around him. He swallows my moan with a kiss at the same time I feel his muscles tense. With one final thrust, Nash finds his release too.

Eight

"Well, that was fun," I mumble into Nash's chest, the light dusting of hair tickling my cheeks.

"Fun would be one word. Sensational would be another," he says before pulling me closer, his lips brushing the top of my head.

As he pulls the comforter over us, I tease, "I didn't think cuddling was part of the benefits."

We laugh together, our breathing still hot and heavy.

I still feel like my heart rate is skyrocketing and the most amazing sex I've ever had has been over for at least ten minutes. When I pictured Nash in bed, I never pictured that. Someone soft and gentle all while being the sexy caveman I thought he could be.

Now that I have a moment to look around, I am somehow surprised at the size of his bedroom. Aside from the fact that I think we are cuddling on an actual cloud plucked from the sky, he has two nightstands next to his bed and a dresser directly in front of us with another huge TV on it. To the left of us is what looks like another living room. Small fireplace, a black leather loveseat, a chair with a coffee table in the middle, and a tall cream cat tower. It looks like the perfect little reading or writing nook. The two doors I can only assume are another bathroom or possibly a walk-in closet. Who am I kidding? If you had this room and didn't have a walk-in closet, you would be a complete idiot.

"I know I keep saying this, but I do think I should go home now."

A sharp inhale from Nash tells me that we're about to start arguing again, so I push myself to a seated position while holding the bedsheet over my bare body.

I open my mouth to explain, but he says, "If that's what you want, I can call you a car. You can also keep the sweats."

I giggle before bending down, placing a light kiss on his perfectly smooth lips. "I was planning on keeping them. I just don't want there to be any confusion about what this is."

Nash places his arm behind his head, "And what is this?"

"Sex. Just sex. Amazing sex, but only sex. We couldn't even get through a movie without finding something to argue about—"

"Because you acted super uptight when I asked you a simple question."

"Uptight? Just because I didn't want to answer one prying question doesn't make me uptight!"

When Nash's square jaw clenches, I groan in frustration. "See! Another argument. We should just have a rule that says we're not allowed to talk to each other."

Nash's eyebrows shoot up. "Now that's not a bad idea."

My mouth drops in horror. "It was a joke, you jerk! You seriously—"

"Oh, calm down." Nash sits up, bringing his knees to his chest and draping his arms around them. "I meant having rules. As you said, this is sex but you can't deny you had a good time with me at the bar. What if instead of this only being about sex, we just made some rules instead?"

Pulling the sheet tighter around me, I chew on my lip. "What kind of rules?"

"That's the beauty of it. We can both come up with a few. Here," Nash reaches down to grab his phone from his jeans and I'll be honest, I did look at the sliver of bare butt under the sheet. "What should our first rule be?"

I guess this isn't the worst idea ever. I tap my chin and begin to think. "No personal questions. Like you can ask about my hobbies and whatever, but my life is a closed book to you."

He grunts in frustration before his fingers move over the keyboard. "Fine. Number two—"

"We're not exclusive."

His face freezes. "Are you trying to tell me that you're planning on having sex with other people?"

"Well, no. I mean, I don't know." I run my hands through my messy hair. "I just mean that we're both still on dating apps, so we should keep our options open."

"All right," he says slowly, "but if that's a rule, then so is open communication. If you meet someone and think they are the one, you tell the other person."

"Deal. Number four, no late-night booty calls. I usually am in bed by ten and I'm not doing the walk of shame because you can't control yourself."

Nash's dimple comes out and he nods as he continues typing. "Why do I feel like you are the one making all the rules? I thought this was supposed to be a team decision."

"By all means," I say, gesturing with my hands for him to say something brilliant and wise.

"Number five, I would like to hang out before sex—"

"That's called a date," I say flatly.

"I don't mean a date. I mean I don't want to be confined to these four walls. Friends with benefits without being friends can still hang out together without it being a date."

Crossing my arms in front of my chest, I lick my lips. Maybe this will be good. If I don't find anyone on those dating apps, then Nash can be the one I drag along to all my Christmas festivities. Mila would much rather spend time with Trey than walk through the neighborhood light show with me for the fifth year in a row.

"I accept your rule," I say. "Do you think five is enough?"

Nash leans over to show me the list and I can't help but laugh. It looks a little silly when I see it all written down.

Friends With Benefits Without Being Friends rules:

1. Don't ask Tatum any questions at all. Like, ever. Seriously.

2. We are definitely not exclusive. It's just sex, right?

3. If you do start something with someone, just tell the other person. Don't be shady.

4. No late-night booty calls. Princess Tatum needs her sleep.

*5. Not-a-date dates can and
will be had before sexual in-
tercourse takes place.*

"Nash!" I playfully swat his shoulder. "You wrote the most ridiculous things."

"Hey, you're the one who came up with the rules. Don't hate the stenographer." We both chuckle as Nash clicks his phone shut and puts it back on his nightstand.

"Wait, I have one more rule." I place my hand out and wait for him to hand me the phone. When I type it and show it to him, I have trouble reading his reaction.

6. No sleepovers.

He nods once before taking it from me. It seems like he's unhappy with the rule, but I'm not sure why.

"You sure you want to leave?" he asks in a soft voice.

"Did you not just read rule number six?"

He shrugs, "Well, I know it's past your bedtime, but I think Frosty the Snowman is on at eleven thirty."

I look over my shoulder at the clock. "That's thirty minutes away. What will we do while we wait?"

Nash tackles me back onto the bed. "I think we can find something fun to do, don't you?"

In my version of the walk of shame, I'm slumping back to my house at one forty-five after getting a ride home, paid for by Nash. I tried to refuse his money, but he made another rule.

7. When Nash wants to pay
the bill, he gets to pay the bill.

I said it wasn't fair and tried to delete the rule, but he said since it was already typed out there was nothing I could do. Due to the late hour, I let it go. A yawn escapes my lips as I let myself into the dark house. Before heading upstairs, I make sure the front door is locked and the alarm is on. I leave my heels by the front door and groan at how incredibly stupid I look in guy sweats with black heels and a dress thrown over my arm. I know I need a shower, but I don't think I could physically stand up the entire time if I tried. I think just washing my face and going to bed seems to be the best decision.

Exhaustion must be affecting my hearing because I don't know how I didn't hear the noise. The bathroom door is cracked, so I push it open only to find a bare-assed Trey, dripping wet and full-on thrusting into my roommate while in the shower. I'm frozen in time for a second before I register what I'm seeing. When Trey and I make direct eye contact, I shut the door as fast as possible, run into my room, lock the door, and will myself to sleep. The only problem is every time I close my eyes, I can see Trey standing with his hands on her hips while he moves back and forth. I make a pretend gagging motion as I shut off my light and pull my comforter over my head.

Nine

Waking up, I pray that last night was a dream. Not the amazing sex part, but the walking-in-on-my-roommate-and-her-boyfriend-going-at-it-in-the-shower part. The shower we share! I listen carefully and when I don't hear anything, I roll out of bed and quickly dress, pulling on some jeans but keeping my black sweatshirt on. Is it wrong that I love the way Nash smells? All man and sweat and sex. My eyes flutter shut as I remember last night: Nash's fingers gripping my waist as his teeth scraped down my neck. My back arching off the bed when Nash hit that oh-so-perfect spot. The noises he made as he came completely undone.

My eyes shoot open when a brief flash of Mila and Trey enters my brain. I should take a shower, but I'm not stepping into that room until I can clean every inch. I know Mila and Trey have sex. They do it all the time. Sometimes I even hear them through the wall and am forced to put on my noise-canceling headphones. However, seeing it with my own two eyes is a totally different story.

Carefully and quietly heading downstairs, I grab my laptop bag and fill it with my laptop, charger, and headphones. After disabling the house alarm, I slip out and take a giant breath. The air is much colder than I thought so I cough a little, but at least it is clean air. Not air tainted with Trey's bare ass.

There's a small coffee shop around the corner from our house that has the best lattes. As I make my way there, I use the collar of my jacket to block out the wind. Once I finally arrive, I run my hand through my hair to untangle some knots, order the biggest coffee I can afford, and sit down in a plush oversized chair near the window. Pulling over a small table, I set it up in front of me and get out my laptop. Powering it up, my mouse hovers over the tab for my book until I decide to click it. My eyes scan over the page, not sure what to do. I could reread it for the millionth time and make more edits or I could just delete the whole thing. Personally, I love my book but that doesn't mean other people will. Gah! Why is this so hard?

My phone vibrates in my coat pocket and I pull it out to find a message from Mila.

M: OMG! I AM SOOO EMBARRASSED! I was so drunk last night that I completely forgot you saw us in the shower! I am so sorry! I wanted to talk to you this morning but you already left:(

T: It's okay. I was just ... stunned? Surprised?
Traumatized?

M: Please let me make this up to you! I didn't
mean to practically run you out of the house. I
just assumed your date went well and that you
weren't coming home.

T: Mila, relax. I just went out to get some work
done. I'll be home later and we can do wine and
pizza?

M: Hell Effing Yes!

Putting my phone away, I grab my headphones and plug them into
my laptop. After I select a classical playlist on my Spotify, I stare at
my words. It doesn't even have a title yet so I just keep referring to it
as The Book. How is it possible that I was able to write 71,000 words
but can't come up with a simple title?

My vision starts to blur after five minutes of staring at the same
sentence. Since no new words are coming to mind, I conclude that
today is not the day for me to work on it. I'm a firm believer in

letting the words flow through me and if I force them, it will just be a waste of time. Opening a new tab, I start the mundane process of job searching. Not only is my current job boring, but the articles I'm told to review are stupid and pointless. Plus, I think my boss desperately needs to get laid. No one is that unhappy and unpleasant all the time. I mean, do people care whether they should read a blog about dying your hair with highlighters? Trust me, I wish I could make this stuff up.

Page after page of job listings for a wannabe writer fill my screen. The only problem is they all are offering significantly less money than I make right now. I hate that I'm the kind of person who is stuck in a soulless job just so she can pay the bills. I know that if I needed help, I could always ask my parents, but that is strictly not an option I'm willing to consider. The only way I will ever ask for their help is if I'm living on the street, and even then it would be questionable.

When my phone vibrates again, I push my laptop away from me. I need a break anyway. My brow furrows at the random number illuminating my screen. Normally I would ignore the call, but it has my area code.

"Hello?"

"Tatum? Hi! Hi! How are you?" Nash stutters.

I pull the phone away from my ear and stare at the screen. Then I put it back to my ear. "Nash? How the hell did you get my number?"

Nash nervously chuckles. "Um, you gave it to me."

"No, I didn't."

"Yes, you did. After we," he clears his throat. "You took my phone and put your info in my contacts. That's the only reason your name in my phone is 'Tatum: AKA the greatest person alive.'"

Brief memories of me holding Nash's iPhone in my hand during my after-sex-euphoric-state come to mind and I internally groan. "That is super embarrassing. Feel free to change that name."

"Like hell I will. I just wanted to call and check in."

I hear the constant rap of shoes and I'm pretty sure Nash is pacing back and forth. Is he nervous?

"Oh, well, I'm good. I'm just doing some work." After a few moments of silence, "How are you?"

"Great! Great. All good."

The pacing has stopped and apparently so has the conversation.

When the silence seems never-ending, I clear my throat. "I should probably get back—"

"There's a pop-up Christmas bar downtown," he almost shouts.

"Yeah. I heard about it. Sounds like a lot of fun."

"Do you, I mean maybe we could, I just think—"

"Are you asking me to go to the pop-up bar with you, Nash?" I ask. Ever since I've met him, he's been the embodiment of cool, calm, and collected. This Nervous-Nellie attitude has me thrown.

"Yes. Well, only if you want to. I'm heading to work soon, but I'm free tomorrow night. I thought since you're all into Christmas that it would be a cool thing to do together. Not together together, just like, together. As in hanging out."

A smile spreads across my face and I can almost picture Nash running his hand nervously through his hair as sweat starts to form along his hairline. This is quite entertaining.

I lower my voice. "Nash, are you nervous right now?"

"What? Why would I be nervous?" he squeaks.

"I'm not sure. You've already seen me naked, so I think you should be able to ask me to hang out and not start sweating."

His nervous laughter has me biting the inside of my cheek.

I suppose I've tortured him long enough. "Pick me up at eight. I'll text you my address."

When we hang up, I hold the phone against my chest. Why can't I stop smiling? Maybe it was just how funny the conversation went. Yeah, let's go with that. I turn my attention back to job searching for only a few minutes until my coffee is gone. Then I pack up and head back home, praying Trey has pants on this time.

To make Mila laugh, I open the front door and shout, "Tatum is entering the front door now. Please make sure all private parts are covered and put away."

Trey's laugh echoes through the hallway and I find Mila baking cookies in the kitchen. Not paying attention, I stumble over the black duffel bag sitting in the middle of the entryway.

"Ouch! What is Trey's bag doing in the middle of the hallway?" I mumble.

"I am so so so so sorry! I don't think I can apologize enough. I made snickerdoodle cookies for you. With red and green sprinkles. I didn't even try the dough. Every single one is for you." Mila's eyebrows are pinched and her lips are chapped as if she's been gnawing on them, her nervous habit.

"Mila!" I walk over and pull her in a tight hug. "Was it ideal for me to see your boyfriend's ass? No, not really. But it's okay! I promise! You don't need to feel bad, but I will take a cookie. Or four."

We both giggle as I pull away and select the biggest cookie on the tray. It's warm and gooey and I think a moan slips from my lips. Mila has always been a talented baker and I thank God for that every day.

"They're Jules's cookies," she whispers.

Surprised, I stop chewing, realizing she's right. "I haven't made these in—"

"I know." Mila touches my arm. "But it's Christmas time. I think she would want you to have some. And no offense, but we both know you can't bake."

"Am I allowed to leave the bedroom yet?" Trey hollers.

Mila's shoulders rise. "I told him to stay hidden until it was safe."

I laugh before shouting back, "Only if your backside is securely covered."

"You say that like I don't have a fantastic ass," Trey teases as he rounds the corner and tries to grab a cookie. Mila swats his hand and he pretends to be injured.

"I've seen better." I shrug.

Later that night, after Trey leaves, Mila and I order pizza and uncork a bottle of Riesling. Tonight's movie is *Home Alone* and we are determined to get through at least two movies before we pass out from the wine. We're sitting on the couch, me on the left and Mila on the right, with our legs tucked under us and sharing a blanket.

Mila's foot nudges mine. "You never did tell me about last night. Was the date bad?"

I choke on my wine and start laughing, remembering Beau. "Bad is one word for it. He said he hates Christmas. How could I seriously date someone who hates the best time of the year?"

"Sounds like someone who is destined to be alone," she says in solidarity.

"Plus, he was, like, shoving the fact that he had money down my throat. His car looked like he was one of the Kardashians, he took me to probably the fanciest restaurant in the city, and he ordered one of the most expensive bottles of wine."

"Ew," Mila says before finishing her glass. Without even asking, she grabs my glass and refills them both. This is why I love her. "Well, if the date was so bad, why did you come home so late?"

I open my mouth but freeze. I didn't put too much thought into if I was going to tell Mila about Nash or not. Being my best friend, she naturally hates him for being a jerk on our first date. Maybe I could just tell her I went to a bar after. That wouldn't be a total lie. Looking into her gigantic, almost Disney-like chocolate eyes, I realize that I can't lie to her. I've never lied to her and I'm not starting now.

"I hooked up with someone."

Her eyes widen and she pauses mid-drink. "I'm sorry. What did you just say?"

I take a rather large gulp before continuing. "After the awful date, I went to a bar close by and ran into someone I know. We got to talking and hooked up."

She gestures with her hands for me to continue but I shake my head. "That's it."

"That is not it!" she says in disbelief. "There is no way that my little Tater Tot went out and had a one-night stand and is this casual about it!"

"Your little baby isn't so little anymore. It wasn't a big deal. It was just sex."

That's all it was. Just sex. No feelings. I just need to keep repeating that over and over in my head.

"Just sex, huh? Was he good?" Mila wiggles her eyebrows.

"I can't even think of a word amazing enough to describe last night," I rejoice while holding up three fingers.

"Three times! Holy shit! Maybe this mystery man can give Trey some pointers. Do I get to know him or was it truly a one-time thing?"

Biting my lip, I debate on revealing Nash's identity. It would be nice to tell her, but then I would have to explain our dynamic. I'm not sure if I'm in the right mental state for that.

"Maybe tomorrow. Right now, I need more wine."

Ten

Since Nash is taking me to a Christmas-themed bar, I have to dress the part. The temperature has dropped and snow is in the forecast, so I grab my candy cane fleece-lined leggings out of my drawer. They are pretty thin and can easily pass for tights, so I pull a long-sleeved black dress over my head and slip into my black boots. I curl my hair and use dry shampoo to add some volume before I apply my eye shadow: a mixture of reds, silvers, and grays. The final touch on my outfit is my big and obnoxious wreath earrings. Green, fuzzy wreaths that have teeny tiny ornaments and bows on them. Super ridiculous and super amazing.

"And where do you think you're going?" Mila leans against my door frame, crossing her arms over her chest. "You look like our advent calendar just threw up."

"I'm choosing to take that as a compliment." Grabbing my black purse off the floor, I toss my phone in while making sure my wallet and house key are still in it.

Mila taps her foot on the floor. "Are you going to tell me or make me guess?"

Exhaling softly, I turn to face her. "It's a long story, but I'm going to hang out with the guy from the other night."

"The loser with the expensive wine and probably tiny—"

"No! Gross! The guy I hooked up with after him."

"Oh!" Her eyes light up. "Mystery man. Do I get to know his name yet?"

The thing is, I know Mila and I know she is going to want every single detail, down to the positions we did it in. I check the time on my phone and see that Nash won't be here for another fifteen minutes. I guess we have time.

"It's, um, Nash. We ran into each other and have come to the decision that we are friends with benefits—without being friends."

Her amused expression drops and she just stares at me, mouth open and brow furrowed. "I'm not even going to pretend I know what that means."

"Well, sex. We can't stand each other, but the sex is mind-blowingly fantastic."

"But you're getting ready to go out on a date with him right now?" She gestures to my outfit. "Why does his name sound so familiar?"

"No, no. This is not a date. We have these rules and according to the rules, we can hang out before we—well, you know. This way it doesn't feel so cheap and dirty."

Mila wrinkles her nose and tilts her head to the side. "So, it's a date."

"It's not a date! I don't want to date him. We have nothing in common. However, we both enjoy going out and doing things, and this way we don't have to do things alone."

"And you're not friends? Wait a minute! Is this the asshole from Sunny's?"

"Um, yes, but it's okay. And we're more like acquaintances." I smile, hoping she will end this conversation.

"Yeah, because that makes sense," she scoffs.

"This is why I didn't want to tell you."

Mila pushes herself off the frame and stands up straight, "Why? Because I would try to understand what's happening?"

"No, because I don't know how to explain it. I know how crazy it sounds, but so far it seems to be working. I have no desire to date Nash, but I'm not giving up the best sex of my life. We have an agreement. Rules. We're not exclusive, so I am going to continue with the dating apps per your Christmas wish."

"Rules?"

"Yes. No sleepovers, personal questions are kept to a minimum, and we are not dating."

I check my phone again and see that Nash should be here any minute. Placing my purse over my shoulder, I can't help the pang I feel in my chest when I see Mila's face fall.

"Mila, it's fine. I promise. This is a good thing. It's just temporary and it's supposed to be something fun."

She sighs. "I just don't want you to get hurt or get your hopes up that Nash is suddenly going to be some amazing guy,"

"I won't," I say, kissing her cheek and squeezing past her. After shrugging into my puffy black coat, I blow a kiss goodbye and head outside. I'm momentarily blinded by harsh headlights shining in my face, but when I get closer to the black BMW, I find Nash standing by the passenger door.

"Of course, you would drive a BMW," I tease as he shuts the door behind me.

"And of course, you would ridicule me over it. How's your hand?" Nash nods towards the bandage on my hand after the car is on the road.

"It's doing really well. The stitches have started dissolving and it's not too painful anymore."

"That's good. Are you cleaning it twice a day? And not just with water, but soap too?" Nash is using his professional doctor voice and I try my best not to roll my eyes.

"Yes, Dr. Anderson. Shocker, but I can read and follow directions."

The drive downtown is quick as we listen to different pop remixes of Christmas classics. We find a spot in a parking garage before heading out into the cold. I pull my coat tighter around me and Nash pops up the collar of his yellow pea coat. Sliding his hand around my waist, we huddle close together. Turning into Market Square, our eyes find a black door with mistletoe hanging above it.

"I think this is it," Nash says as he knocks on the door.

My eyes travel up to the green leaves hanging over our heads and I wonder if it would be weird if I kissed Nash. Maybe just a quick peck on the cheek? You know, for tradition's sake. We agreed to all benefits, so doesn't that cover kissing? Before I can make a move, Nash's lips brush mine.

"Mistletoe," he says with a smirk.

The door opens to a buff man in a very tight T-shirt. Nash shows him something on his phone, and the man nods and lets us pass. The whole secret-society vibe is very James Bond. Once we're inside, Nash takes my coat and places his hand on my lower back, guiding me through a dark hallway. When we make it to the next room, green and red lights fill my vision. Every inch of the bar is covered in either mistletoe, Christmas trees, garlands, or some other kind of holiday decoration. A cut-out of the Grinch stands next to the bar and there's a fake snow machine in the corner. A shriek of excitement escapes my lips as I jump up and down. Nash chuckles at my reaction, but I don't care. This is possibly the best place I have ever been to.

We sit down at a tabletop across from the bar and I grab the menu. The drinks are all holiday-themed: Ho-Ho-Hot Toddy, Jingle Juice, Red-Nosed Rum Punch, Santa-gria, White Christmas, Gin and Tiding, Getting Blitzen, and Mrs. Claus's Cosmo.

"These are hysterical!" I shout to Nash over the remix of "Jingle Bell Rock" that is booming from a jukebox.

"I figured you'd like it," Nash says with a wink.

An elf stops at our table and asks for our order.

"I'll have Santa-gria."

Nash chuckles. "I'll have Ho-Ho-Hot Toddy."

The elf nods and vanishes into the crowd.

"I don't think I've seen you smile like this before," Nash mutters.

Looking around, I'm pretty sure my smile somehow gets bigger. "This place is seriously amazing. Did you see the guy dressed like Papa Elf?"

He nods while running a hand through his hair. For the first time tonight, I take a moment to really look at him. His hair, which usually has that fresh-out-of-bed vibe, seems like it was styled perfectly. His button-down blue striped shirt fits him deliciously, but the horny teenager in me can't wait for him to take it off.

He wants sex tonight, right? That's why we're hanging out. I didn't even consider the possibility of him just wanting to go to a bar without having sex after. I freaking shaved my legs for this. One way or another, he's getting naked at the end of tonight.

The elf drops off our drinks and I all but chug mine. It's delicious and goes down way too easily.

"Good thing you have a driver tonight. Want me to order you another?" Nash asks, gesturing to my empty glass. I lick my lips before nodding. His eyes almost pop out of his head when my tongue darts out of my mouth. Okay, he definitely is thinking about sex too.

After we've been at the bar for about an hour (and many drinks later), someone turns on the fake snow machine.

"Snow!" I shout, jumping off my stool and spinning around. "Snow is the best part of winter! I wish it would snow. Everything magical happens when it snows."

Nash's arms wrap around my waist and I turn to him, placing mine around his neck.

"You are drunk," he informs me and I dramatically shake my head side to side, causing my wreath earrings to smack me in the face.

"I like these," Nash adds, tapping my earrings.

"And I like these," I say as my hands fall to his abs. He laughs as I push away and continue spinning in the fake snow.

"Love your outfit!" some girl walking by says and I thank her.

"She likes my outfit," I shout in Nash's ear. "You didn't compliment me on my outfit." I jut out my lower lip. "I wore my favorite leggings."

Nash's dimple appears. "I love that outfit. It's very festive."

"It would look better on your bedroom floor," I tease and jump up and down to "Santa Claus is Coming to Town."

The elf walks by us and Nash stops him.

"I love your ears!" I shout and point to my ears. He nods and forces a smile. A deep V forms between my brows at his response. When he walks away, I lean into Nash. "He's not very jolly."

"No, he's not," Nash agrees before grabbing my hand. I blindly follow him and frown when we're outside.

"Wait, I'm not done. I want to try Getting Blitzen!"

"You're blitzed enough," he laughs and I laugh too. His smile is so genuine and natural. It's beautiful.

"Can we just go back for one more drink?" I whine, holding one finger up in front of his face.

He grabs my finger and pulls it away, "We can either go back in for one drink or we can go back to my place and—"

"Say no more!" I shout, grabbing his hand and trying to run back to his car. "You're not helping. At least walk a little faster."

He chuckles as he picks up his pace. When he steps closer, I lose my balance and feel as if I'm falling in slow motion. Strong arms wrap around my waist and save me from my imminent death. I'm pressed against Nash's hard chest and I look up at him through my lashes. I think he's about to kiss me when a snowflake falls on my nose.

I turn my attention to the sky and smile. "It's snowing."

When I open my eyes, I'm confused. How did I get in a car? My eyes drift over and find Nash steering us through what I'm assuming is downtown.

"What happened?" I mumble and he turns off the radio.

"After you sang about the snow, we were hugging and you fell asleep on my chest. I carried you back to the car and now we're almost back at your place."

How the hell does someone fall asleep on someone's chest while they are standing up? I didn't have that much to drink. Wait, maybe I did. A shy smile falls over my face thinking about Nash carrying me.

"Wait, why are we going to my house? I thought we were going back to yours."

Nash glances at me before looking back at the road. "A rule I pretty much live by is not to sleep with someone who is comatose."

My face falls and I let out an exhausted sigh. Running my hands through my hair, I want to smack myself. Nash is probably pissed that I got drunk and ruined his night. Looks like acquaintances with benefits is going to be over before it even starts.

"I'm so sorry. I didn't think—"

"Why are you sorry?"

I shrug. "I got drunk and probably ruined your night. I'm sorry if I ruined whatever this is." I gesture between us before pressing my head against the window and watching the snowflakes fall. I thought snow was supposed to be magical. Where's the magic?

"You think you ruined my night?" When I hear the smile in Nash's voice, I turn back towards him. "You were a freaking hit. I can't remember the last time I had that much fun. I'm not taking you back to your house because I want to end things. I just figured you'd be more comfortable in your own bed."

"Oh."

I'm not prepared for Nash's immediate stop, so my head flings back into the headrest. "What was that?"

Nash puts the car in park, unbuckles his seat belt, and turns to me. "Why do you do that?"

"Do what?"

"Always think the worst. I thought you were supposed to be this holly-jolly person."

I frown at his comment. "I am holly jolly, dammit! I just assumed—"

"Well, cut it out. Stop assuming shit. I really did have a lot of fun tonight." Nash's finger grazes my cheek before he pushes a lock of hair behind my ear. "I was at a cool bar with a beautiful girl. What more could a guy ask for?"

My lips part as I lean into Nash's hand. I look behind me and back at him. "Ever had sex in a car before?"

Nash's eyebrows raise in question. "Is there a specific reason you're asking? I'm only saying that because there's a list of rules that says no personal questions, and that feels pretty personal."

I don't even try to hide the fact that I'm rolling my eyes. "You seriously are one of the most annoying people I have ever met."

"Likewise," Nash agrees before his lips crash against mine.

Not wanting to waste any time, I place my hands on his chest, pushing him back. When he furrows his brow in confusion, I shimmy into the backseat.

"Tatum," he says, looking at me in the rearview mirror, "do you really think this is a good idea?"

"You're just going to leave me back here all alone?" I pretend to pout.

"You're going to be the death of me." More logically, Nash steps out of the car before climbing into the back and I manage to strip off my coat and dress while I wait. His lips find mine again, greedy and wanting. My fingers instantly find his belt when a loud thump scares the living crap out of us. Nash bites my lip, drawing blood before turning towards the bright light shining in the window.

"Roll down your window!" the police officer demands, lowering his flashlight.

Nash shifts his body so he's covering me and does as he's told. "Good evening, officer. What seems to be the problem?"

I bury my face in his back to avoid laughing.

The officer clears his throat. "This is public property and you two look rather old to be fooling around in a car together. I need you to move along."

"Right away. Sorry, officer," Nash says with a hint of laughter.

When we're alone again, I quickly get dressed and scurry back to the passenger seat. I think Nash and I are both stunned because we don't say anything for a few minutes.

"Well, that's a first for me," he says before bursting out laughing. I follow suit, tears streaming down my face from the ridiculousness of the situation.

"I cannot believe that just happened," I exclaim. "You know, if we would've just gone back to your place, we could've avoided the whole ordeal."

"And there's my girl."

Eleven

I'm currently lying in bed and staring at my ceiling while reminiscing on what a cluster last night was. Let's recount the events, shall we? I got drunk and made a fool of myself, started another fight with Nash, and tried to seduce him in his car only to get caught by the police! Rubbing the sleep from my eyes, I wonder if I just focus enough if I can go back and time and redo the entire night.

My phone chimes, indicating I have a text message, and I blindly reach for it. My entire body flinches when I accidentally knock over the water glass that was sitting on my nightstand. Rolling over, I pick the glass up from the floor and set it back in its original place before grabbing my phone.

> N: Last night was an adventure. Want to try the actual benefits part of our relationship tonight?

> T: Relationship? Is it possible for one to be in a relationship with a non-friend?

I chuckle at my response but then stop. There's this weird feeling in the pit of my stomach and I'm not sure how to describe it. When I first met Nash, I couldn't stand him. However, when I ran into him at the bar after my disaster-of-a-date with Beau, something clicked between us. Yes, the sex between us was amazing, but I'm not talking about that. It was oddly fun to bicker back and forth with Nash. I'll admit I was super annoyed when he asked me questions about my family, but part of me wanted to answer him honestly. Maybe we are becoming friends?

Oh, crap! I hope he knows I meant that last text as a joke.

> T: Haha

There. Maybe that will soften my words. After five minutes with no response, I force myself out of bed and start getting ready for the day ahead. I'm just finishing applying my eyeliner when my phone dings.

> N: I need a break. Play hooky with me today? Downtown has a beautiful ice rink that should be practically empty during the workday.

Ice skating? Isn't that something couples do? I mean, I guess acquaintances can ice skate together too. I should say no, but a bonus of working from home is I can clock in and out whenever I want, as long as I work the required number of hours. Damn Nash for knowing my weakness for holiday activities.

T: Are you picking me up or am I meeting you there?

Opening my closet, I tap my chin while scanning through my clothes. I'm wearing black leggings with my Santa-themed knee-length socks, but what Christmas sweater should I wear with it? I grab my light blue sweater that hits mid-thigh. Three snowmen (or women) dance on the front of it and above them in big bold white letters reads,"'Chilling with my Snowmies." By the time I've grabbed my coat, purse, and boots, Nash's car is already in the driveway.

The outdoor ice-skating rink is located at PPG Place in the heart of downtown. A gigantic and beautiful Christmas tree sits in the center of the rink where people stop and take pictures. I bite my lip so I don't admit to Nash that he was right. There's hardly a line to pay for tickets and rent your skates. The downside of not waiting very long is I have less time to freak out. I've had more than enough stitches for a lifetime and don't have a good track record with skating. What if I fall and cut my finger or my hand? Not only will that be humiliating, but it will also probably make Nash never want to come near me again. I swear I am the clumsiest person I know.

Absentmindedly, I run my thumb over the scar on my middle finger while Nash pays for our tickets. I offered to pay, and even tried to hand him my credit card, but he referred back to our rules.

"You okay?" Nash asks after his skates are on his feet. I frantically nod while trying to lace mine up. For some reason, my stupid hands won't stop shaking, which makes grasping the laces almost impossible.

"Here." Nash kneels before me, placing my foot on his lap. "We don't have to go skating if you don't want to. I just figured you would love it."

"I will," I say a little too loudly, still rubbing my scar.

After Nash finishes lacing my skates, he sits back on his knees. He makes a gesturing motion with his hands and I get the feeling he's not going to let me walk away without explaining.

"Fine. The last time I went skating, I came with Trey and Mila. They did their couple stuff and I ended up falling on my ass and slicing my finger with my skate. I honestly have no idea how it even happened."

Nash frowns. "Which finger?"

I smile and place my middle finger in his face. He chuckles before taking it and examining my scar. His lips brush the raised skin before he stands up, offers me his hands, and pulls me to my feet. I wobble as Nash helps me find my center. Holding my hand, he guides me out to the rink. After showing our tickets to the employee at the entrance, Nash and I step onto the ice. Instinctively, I tighten my grip on Nash's hand as my other grabs the side railing. When Nash laughs at me, I try to pull my hand free of his, but he won't let me.

He leans close to my ear. "I promise I won't let you fall. Just trust me. I am a doctor, after all."

Slowly releasing my grip on the wall, I begin to move my feet. Immediately I stumble, but Nash catches me. He plants a kiss on my nose before helping me stand up again. After a few more minutes of me almost falling and Nash catching me, I'm able to hold my weight and skate on my own. I get so comfortable that I even glide away from Nash, forcing him to chase me.

"So, how were you able to play hooky today?" I ask. "I thought doctors had to work all the time."

Nash shakes his head. "God, no! I've been at the hospital for a while now and have a pretty easy schedule. Another doctor needed to switch some days around this week, so I was able to have a free day."

"Interesting. And there were no other friends with benefits you wanted to bring skating?"

He narrows his eyes. "I can barely handle you, let alone another girl. Anyway, are you not going to tell me how you were able to take the day off from your mysterious day job I'm not allowed to ask about?"

The cold air stings my face and I have to squint against the wind. I surprisingly have a weird urge to be honest with him instead of fighting with him.

"I'm a writer. Well, kind of. I work for this online site that reviews blogs. I read stupid blogs all day and decide which ones are worth promoting through the site. If I'm being honest, I hate it. It's stupid and a monkey could do it, but it pays the bills."

"And that's why you got mad at me the other night."

Exhaling sharply, I answer, "Yeah. I don't usually like talking about it because when I do, people tell me to quit and find something I'm passionate about."

"Why don't you do that?"

I turn to look at him and am surprised to find him watching me. He's genuinely interested in what I have to say.

"Because what I'm passionate about will never make me money. I have looked for other jobs, but none of them pay as well as *Starz Weekly*. I just kind of feel like I'm stuck."

"Wait, what do you mean you'll never make any money doing what you're passionate about?"

I just shrug, but he continues, "I thought you wrote a novel."

A shy smile spreads across my lips. "I did. Kind of."

"What does that mean?"

"Well, I wrote it. I just am not very happy with the ending."

He nods slowly. "So you want to be an author?"

"Um, yeah. I would love to be an author and not some sell-out who works for some stupid website."

"So do it."

"What? Nash, it's not that easy. I tried sending the book out to some agents a while back, but nothing came of it. I've been toying with the idea of self-publishing, but..." My words trail off. I don't have anything else to say. This is the most I've openly talked about my book in a very long time. With someone who isn't Mila.

"But what?"

My eyes fall to the ice below us, carved up by the other skaters. "But self-publishing is risky. What if I spend all this time creating what I think is an amazing book for other people to think it's a waste of paper? Plus, it's a lot of money for me to just throw away. It's just safer not to do it. That's all."

"That's all?" Nash drags me over to the railing to steady me. "I don't believe anything your mind could create would be a waste. You can't just not try, Tatum."

"I did try," I say, a little irritated. "I spent months of my life sending pages to people who gave generic responses about how they didn't like my words. Rejection after rejection takes its toll and I don't think I have it in me to do that crap again."

"But—"

"I'm getting cold," I interrupt, rubbing my arms for dramatic effect.

Seeing I'm done with this conversation, Nash offers me his hand. "Want to get some hot chocolate?"

I take his hand and we exit the rink. Before we can walk back into the storefront to return our skates, Nash pulls me close to him. Taking his phone out of his pocket, he snaps a pic of us: his smile that spreads to his eyes, my closed-lipped smile as I lean my head on his shoulder, and the giant Christmas tree right behind us.

Across the street, we head to Market Square. It's a literal square with different restaurants, coffee shops, and, during the winter months, vendors of handcrafted items. I buy us two hot chocolates and two pretzels from a small shop. When I turn around and run into a mom trying to wrangle four kids, causing me to drop the hot chocolates all over my shoes, Nash buys the replacements. We eat and drink as we explore the booths spread throughout the square. We find ornaments, hot chocolate bombs, keychains, bracelets, and wall art. Nash buys a picture frame with small sticks glued onto it. He lets me know that it will look great on his mantel. That's when I use the opportunity to ask if he wants me to help him find a place for it on his mantel, and that's why we are now practically running back to his car.

❄ ❄ ❄ ❄ ❄

"Today was a lot of fun," I mumble into Nash's mouth as he slams his front door behind us.

"Mm. And the best part, no stitches," he teases as his teeth graze my collarbone.

I shimmy out of my jacket before pushing his off his shoulders. I go to kiss him when he places his hands on my shoulders and stops me. I give him a confused look when I notice he's looking at my shirt.

"I don't know why I'm surprised. That is probably the best holiday sweatshirt I've ever seen."

"Don't say that yet," I pant, sliding my pants down my legs. "You haven't seen the one that makes me look like a Christmas tree."

Nash groans and my hands find his belt. Clothes start flying and just as I'm about to take off my sweater, Nash stops me.

"What?"

"Leave the sweater on," he winks.

I swat his shoulder just before he bends down, tosses me over his shoulder, and takes me into his bedroom.

Twelve

"Thank you," Nash mumbles into my hair before placing a kiss on my head. I'm still panting from the three orgasms I just had.

"Thank you for what?" I ask, my finger drawing circles over his chest as I cuddle my naked body closer to his.

"For being honest with me about wanting to become an author. I know that must have been hard."

Nash can push my buttons like no one else, but he does know when to ease off. I appreciate that about him. The funny thing is, I'm happy I told him. It feels good to say the words out loud. Just like Mila, Nash is trying to encourage me, which is appreciated, but not needed.

A high-pitched meow startles me and the feline I assume to be Smelly Cat jumps on the bed and struts towards me.

"Hi, kitty," I say in a calming voice. I have been wondering when I was going to meet Nash's infamous fur child. Holding my hand out, I wait for Smelly Cat to come closer. When she looks at Nash for approval, he nods with a smile. After a careful examination and decision that my hand is not a danger, she nuzzles into me.

"I think she likes you." Nash chuckles.

Smelly Cat makes her way over to my lap, kneads the blankets to her liking, and plops down on me.

"I mean, your father, who takes care of you day in and day out, is sitting right here, but it's cool if you want to sit on someone who is a total stranger," Nash says in the cat's direction.

"Aw, jealousy isn't a good look on you, sweetheart," I tease and stick my tongue out.

Nash puts on *It's a Wonderful Life* and we watch together in comfortable silence, our naked bodies tangled under the sheets. Nash's fingers brush up and down my spine. I can't remember the last time I felt this happy. When the credits start to roll, I finally get out of bed.

"You're leaving?" Nash asks, leaning against the headboard with one arm propped behind his head.

Spinning in circles, I'm annoyed. "Where's my underwear?"

A wicked smile crosses his face. "I'll debate telling you if you get back in bed."

Rolling my eyes, I use my stern voice. "No. I took the morning off and need to start working soon. Seriously, where the hell are my clothes?"

Walking back out into the living room, I finally find my pants and sweater but still no underwear. When I turn around, Nash has my bra on his head and my panties dangling from his finger.

"Give it back," I demand with a smile.

"What's it worth to you?" Nash challenges, pulling my bra off his head as he approaches me.

"Drinks this weekend? I'll even let you pay," I tease.

"Oh, how generous of you. But that only gets you your bra." Placing my bra in my hands, he turns back to his bedroom.

My mouth hangs open as I debate what to do next. I know he wants me to chase him. I can see it now: I run after him, demanding my panties back, and somehow we end up back in his bed doing the exact thing we were doing only a few hours ago. As much as I would love to go for round two, I do need to go. I decide to get dressed sans underwear, and strut back into the bedroom.

"I'm ready to go," I say as I poke my head in the bedroom, but stutter the last words when I find Nash lying in bed with no covers.

"Are you sure you want to go?" Nash winks.

"Come on, Casanova!" I yell. My willpower is only so strong and if I stay in that room any longer, I won't be leaving at all.

Wednesday morning, I wake to my phone ringing in my ear. At first I think it's part of a dream, so I ignore it and when the noise stops, I slowly start to drift back to sleep. When it starts ringing again, I moan while forcing myself to a sitting position and grabbing it off the nightstand.

It's my mother. I hit ignore. How does she not get the not-so-subtle hint that I don't want to talk to her? I can't even remember the last time I actually answered her call. Maybe a few months ago? Rubbing my hands down my face, I get ready for the workday ahead.

Around noon, I take my thirty-minute lunch break to make a turkey-and-cheese sandwich. I'm about to shove the last bite in my mouth when my phone vibrates in my back pocket. A smile instantly forms on my face as I'm hoping it will be Nash. Wait, why do I want it to be Nash? It's obviously only because of the mind-blowing sex. Yeah, that's definitely what it is. I chew on my lip when I hesitate. Maybe if it is Nash, I shouldn't be so eager to answer it. This is just sex and I wouldn't want him to get the wrong idea.

To say I'm surprised to find the notification is from BeeMine is an understatement. My thumb swipes across the screen to open it.

Tatum! It was great to receive your message. Some craziness at work has kept me pretty busy lately, but I would love to still grab drinks with you if you are available. What's your schedule like this weekend?

Brendon. The architect. I forgot about him and his adorable glasses after the horrible dates I've been on. Now that I think about it, I haven't even opened my dating apps since I started sleeping with Nash.

Brendon,

That sounds lovely. How does Friday night sound?

-T

Just as I'm logging back into work, Brendon messages me saying that he'll pick me up around seven thirty and I send him my address. I want to smile, but every single date I've been on has been such a failure, I don't want to get my hopes up.

I finish my reviews for the day and log out. My plans for this evening include a nice, long bubble bath while drinking a glass of white wine. Those plans slowly begin to evaporate when Trey waltzes through the door.

"How'd you get in? I locked the door," I say from my spot on the couch.

"Mila made me a key. Is she not here yet?" Trey stuffs his hands in his jean pockets and looks down the hall. He has a giant duffel bag on his shoulder, which has me confused.

"No." I click the TV off. "And I was just about to go take a bath, so ..."

"What's on TV?" he asks, dropping the bag and plopping down next to me.

"That was my subtle way of telling you to leave. Anyway, what's in the bag?" I say in a lighthearted voice. I don't want to be rude, but I want him to get out so I can relax in peace.

"Chill, T. Mila should be back soon. Cool if I just wait here?"

My shoulders slump. "I was watching Food Network."

"Sounds delicious." Trey takes the remote from me and clicks the television back on.

When my phone vibrates with a text from Nash, a smile automatically spreads across my face.

> N: Apparently this isn't common knowledge, so I wanted to share the wealth. It is physically impossible to fall on any object and get it lodged into your rectum. Especially when that object is a television remote.

My eyes widen and I can't decide if I'm disgusted or intrigued. First off, how do you get a remote up there? Second, why would you want to put a remote up there? That seems incredibly uncomfortable and not practical at all.

"Something funny?" Trey asks while keeping his eyes on the TV. Gordon Ramsay is making something that looks mouthwateringly delicious.

"Just something my friend texted me."

Wait, did I just call Nash my friend? I guess he kind of is. Weird how that happened.

"Friend like Mila or friend like someone who sees you naked?"

I gently swat his arm. "Trey!"

"What?" He chuckles. "Just so you know, your face says it's the kind of friend you sleep with."

"So what if it is? Nash and I are just hanging out. Nothing serious."

Trey nods but still doesn't meet my eyes.

After thirty seconds of silence, I groan. "What's all the nodding for?"

He finally turns to look at me. "This guy is someone you're just sleeping with?"

I nod.

"And you both have no emotional connection to each other whatsoever?"

I nod again.

"I hate to tell you this, but guys who are just sleeping with someone don't text them random funny things. They usually only text each other times and places."

My mouth opens, but nothing comes out. That's not true. That can't be true.

"It's just sex," I finally say.

"Just sex?"

"Yes. We have rules. Just sex and we're not exclusive. It's the perfect arrangement."

Trey straightens in his seat, seeming more interested in our conversation. "So you're both seeing other people?"

"Well, I don't know if he is. I just made a date for Friday night—"

"And you'll tell him about this date?"

"I ..."

Trey starts to nod again. "And there it is. If this was truly just sex, you wouldn't hesitate to tell him about some other guy you were going out with."

"I'm home!" Mila shouts before I have a chance to say anything else.

"Babe!" Trey shouts, getting off the couch and pulling Mila to him.

They both disappear out the door, Mila telling me she'll be back later.

Wait! What just happened? What did Trey mean, *if* this was truly just sex? Of course, it's just sex! Nash and I have rules. We are just having sex. Nothing else.

Thirteen

Halfway through my workday on Thursday, my phone dings with a text.

> N: Was Christmas shopping and passed this little bakery. They had cupcakes that were just as obnoxious as your earrings. Naturally, I bought a dozen.

> T: Now, how obnoxious are we talking? Because I have some pretty awesome earrings you've never even seen.

N: Show them to me? I don't work tonight and
if you come over, I won't be forced to eat twelve
cupcakes by myself.

Chewing on my fingernail, I remember what Trey said yesterday. *I hate to tell you this, but guys who are just sleeping with someone don't text them random funny things. They usually only text each other times and places.*

Whatever! Just because we are now becoming friends and texting each other cute things does not mean there are any feelings between us.

I finish my writing for the day, grab my earrings that have cats wearing Santa hats, and use Mila's car to make a quick stop at the supermarket before going over to Nash's. Jeeves sends me up to the penthouse when I walk through the door carrying three overflowing bags.

"Can I help you, Miss Tatum?"

"I'm good. Thanks, Jeeves." I smile and he tips his hat.

"What's all this?" Nash asks when the elevator doors open. Without thinking, I drop the bags and run into his arms. Lifting me, he buries his face in my neck, inhaling deeply.

"Hi," I murmur, pecking at his lips.

"Hi. That was quite an entrance."

I smack his shoulder and try to get down but his grip tightens.

"I had a dream last night," he says, rubbing his nose against mine.

"And what was this dream about?"

A breath leaves me as he presses my back against the wall. "You were in it."

"Mm-hmm?" I reach for his lips, but he pulls back with a smile.

"And you were very very naked." Pinning me to the wall with his hips, he skims his fingers up my sides and under my blouse.

"I think I like where this is going."

Nash's hands find my breasts, pinching and rolling my nipples through the sheer fabric of my bra.

"Nash," I moan.

"I like it when you say my name. Say it again."

I almost scream his name when he presses his hard length on my throbbing center.

He clears his throat. "As I was saying—"

I grab his face, forcing him to look at me. "If you don't fuck me right now, I—"

I let out a yelp when Nash whips me around and tosses me down on the couch. He climbs up my body and I'm so impatient, I twist my fingers in his shirt and pull him towards me.

"In my dream, we took it slow." He bites my lower lip. "Took our time."

"Thank God we aren't in your dream."

It's like a switch flips and suddenly Nash is tearing off my leggings and panties while my fingers undo his pants. We're acting like horny teenagers and I love it. Once his boxers disappear, I reach down and wrap my hand around his length.

"Tatum," he says through a sharp intake of breath.

Sliding my hand up and down his shaft, I arch my back, pressing my body to his. Nash's eyes shut and his arm that is propping him up tenses.

"Open your eyes," I softly command.

When he does, I drag my other hand between my breasts, down my belly, and only stop once I've reached my target.

A whimper escapes me as I lightly caress myself. Teasing just enough to give Nash his own private show.

"Tatum. Holy—"

I increase my pace, my breathing growing shallow and fast. "I need you, Nash."

Pushing my hand away, Nash lines himself up and I gasp when he fills me completely. I arch my hips to meet him when he places a hand on my chest.

"You feel amazing. So wet and tight, and all for me."

Digging my fingers into his hips, I reach up and find his lips. Our tongues meet as we begin to move. Every thrust hits exactly where I need him and I want more.

"Let me ride you," I whisper as I wrap my legs around his waist.

"Hold on, sweetheart."

Nash pulls me up so he's sitting and I'm now straddling him. His lips nibble down my neck as I twist my fingers into his soft hair. His hands explore every inch of my body, reaching under my sweater and finding their way into my bra. A soft moan escapes my lips as his pace quickens.

"Don't be shy. You know I like hearing you." His voice is husky.

Holding onto his shoulders, I take over. His hands rest on my hips as he leans his head back, watching me. The change in position has me shaking and I can feel how close I am. Nash's tongue licks a path up the column of my neck, his hands sliding around to my ass. A sudden sharp smack has me reeling. Meeting me thrust for thrust, Nash's finger slips down between my cheeks, stroking my back entrance. The most intense sensation swells in my stomach and when my grip tightens on Nash's hair, he moves faster. And faster, until I scream. Like, actually scream. Do people typically scream during sex? Because I sure as hell don't. Just as I'm coming down from my orgasm, Nash's body stiffens underneath me.

Now, I have had good sex before. But what just happened, there aren't even words to describe it. A combination of pleasure and pain that was so mind-blowing, I lost complete control of myself.

"Holy hell," I pant.

"That was—"

"Yeah," I agree.

My leg jerks when I feel fur rub against it. Laughing to myself, I remember Smelly Cat lives here too. If she was in the room the entire time, Nash and I just gave her one hell of a performance.

Nash looks up at me and chuckles. "Did you scream? I clearly am very good at my job."

I swat his chest. "Shut up! I have legit never screamed while orgasming before."

Nash pretends to dust some dirt off his shoulder and I climb off him.

As I'm shimmying into my pants, Nash asks, "That wasn't too much, was it?"

Too much? Is he kidding? Did he not hear me scream?

"What are you talking about, too much?"

He opens his mouth to explain but when he can't find the words, he just shrugs. The only things he could possibly be talking about are the … oh.

"Do you mean the butt smack or the—"

"Yeah. The other thing." He runs a hand through his messy head of hair. "I probably should've asked you before. I just got caught up in the moment."

A smile forms on my face and I take the few steps to him. "I really, really liked what we just did. And if I had any complaints, I would've told you. I promise."

His dimple appears. "Good. Because I really, really liked what we just did, too."

Once we're both re-dressed, we head to the kitchen to grab a drink of water. Nash takes a big gulp from the glass he just filled and hands me the rest.

"You never told me what was in the bags."

Rushing over, I pick up the bags with a big smile plastered on my face. "I decided this place isn't festive enough."

His eyebrows raise. "You decided?"

"Mm-hm."

"You know you don't actually live here, right?"

I roll my eyes. "Minor details. Now, come help me."

After I turn some Christmas music on, I bend down and pull out decoration after decoration before I notice Nash isn't helping. He's hovering above me, lips parted and brow furrowed.

"What are you doing?" I ask.

"I'm trying to figure out if you're genuinely crazy or not."

With a smile on my face, I wrap a strand of tinsel around my neck like a boa and stand up.

Strutting towards him, I move my hips in the most obnoxious way to the music. As I continue to move, I take the tinsel off my neck and wrap it around his.

"You weren't saying that a few minutes ago."

Reaching up, I graze my lips with his. I yelp in surprise when he growls and pulls me closer, devouring my mouth.

Two hours and a bottle of wine later, Nash's apartment looks perfect. White twinkle lights dangle from the ceiling, stockings are secured on garland on the fireplace, and the cutest Christmas hand towels I have ever seen now hang from his stove.

"I suppose this place does look more festive now." Nash gives me a high five, but when I go to pull my hand back, he drags me closer and brushes his lips over mine. "I love it."

"And you know what I would love?" I say, walking my fingers up his chest.

He creases his forehead in question.

Stopping my lips inches from his, I whisper, "A cupcake."

The snow continues falling and by Friday night, the world is covered in a beautiful white blanket. Not sure what Brendon and I are doing tonight, I dress in jeans, my red holiday sweater with a silver reindeer, and black boots. When I hear a knock at the door, I grab my purse and coat.

"Is this the guy you're going on a date with or sleeping with?" Trey asks, leaning against my door frame and blocking me from leaving.

"Move."

He chuckles before letting me out of my room. When I hear Mila open the door, I head down the hallway before she has a chance to scare him off.

"I'm Mila. The roommate. I assume you're the guy who is going to treat my best friend like a queen."

"Brendon. Nice to meet you. Is Tatum here?" he asks after he offers Mila his hand.

"Sorry about her. Just ignore her." I kiss Mila on the cheek and almost push Brendon out the door.

"Make good choices!" Trey yells at our backs.

Sliding on my coat, my eyes scan down Brendon's body. Peacoat over a button-down with nice jeans and winter boots. He opens the passenger side door, helping me into the car.

Once he joins me inside, I turn to him. "I'm sorry about that. Mila gets overprotective sometimes."

He smiles and I reciprocate. "That's all right," he says. "Mila seems like a good friend. And before I forget, you look incredible."

"You look pretty good too. So where are we going tonight?"

Brendon nods towards me. "Is your coat pretty warm?"

Thank God my answer to that question is yes. Although, in true gentlemanly fashion, Brendon brought hand warmers for each of us. We park in a garage downtown and Brendon takes my gloved hand as he leads me to the street. Our date is a snow-filled walk through downtown and I huddle close to Brendon, trying to stay warm. Maybe this was his idea the entire time? Clever man. Our first stop is Point State Park.

"If this at all bores you, please let me know. I don't want to ruin this date by gushing about architecture," he warns.

I playfully swat his arm. "I highly doubt this will be boring. I've been to The Point plenty of times before, but I have no idea what this is."

We stop in front of a small blockhouse and Brendon's smile grows.

"This,"—he opens his arms like he's presenting the house to me—"is Fort Pitt Block House. Probably my favorite architecture in all of downtown."

"And why is that?" I ask, a puff of air coming from my mouth.

"The blockhouse is the only structure left of Fort Pitt, making it the oldest structure in this part of the state. The fort was built in 1764 by the British as a defense against Native American attacks. Later, it was used as a trading post, and then as housing."

"Wow." I take in the building in front of us. "That's incredible."

"Typically you can go inside and look around, but that's only during daylight hours."

"Then I guess we'll have to come back another day," I say with optimism.

Brendon smiles before squeezing my hand. It's a sweet gesture. I try not to focus on the fact that it feels more like friends holding hands than lovers.

"Before we continue the tour, I do want to go see the tree."

My heart flutters at his words. Walking towards the eighty-foot Christmas tree that replaces the Point fountain for the holidays is always on my to-do list over the holidays, but usually gets pushed to the bottom.

"This is amazing! I've never actually gotten to see it up close. There's always so much going on this time of year," I gush.

Brendon turns to me, one eyebrow arched. "Are you ready for me to really geek out?"

I nod enthusiastically. "Definitely!"

He looks down at his shoes as if he's embarrassed. "The location of the fountain used to serve as a connector for the Manchester Bridge, which would sit over the Allegheny River, and the Point Bridge, which would be over the Monongahela River. Both were removed in 1970 to make way for the fountain."

"Wow. That's pretty cool."

He nods, pursing his lips. "Also the tradition of having the Christmas tree here every year started in 1988."

I giggle. "You are a total nerd!"

"The nerdiest." We quietly laugh together. "I think my love of architecture goes along with my love of history."

"Well, I think it's interesting. I've lived here my whole life and never knew any of that."

Brendon gently bumps my shoulder with his. "I went to eight years of college. The number of facts I know about architecture, let alone Pittsburgh architecture, is overwhelming."

Silence falls over us, but it's not uncomfortable. It's peaceful.

Smiling as we admire the tree, Brendon exhales softly. "I can't believe it's taken me this long to come down here. Christmas is my favorite time of the year."

Shut up! He's adorable and likes Christmas too?

"Christmas is your favorite holiday? It's my favorite holiday!" I say a little too loudly and with way too much enthusiasm.

Brendon taps his chin with his finger. "Favorite holiday movie?"

"Easy. How The Grinch Stole Christmas. You?"

"The Grinch? Really? He's so angry and anti-Christmas—"

"But that's only because he was an outsider. Once Cindy Lou showed him that he could be a part of Christmas with people who cared about him, he changed his views. At least, she did in the live-action version."

Brendon holds his hands up in defeat and I smile victoriously. "All right, all right," he says. "It's still no Charlie Brown, though."

The multicolored lights fill our vision and I take the opportunity to rest my head on Brendon's shoulder. Everything about this moment is insanely perfect. Nash would love it.

Wait, what?

Our walking tour of downtown continues, but not for too long. The temperature drops when the snow starts to fall again and Brendon and I escape into a local tavern. The rustic wooden vibe of the bar screams Christmas and we find two plush chairs near the fireplace in the corner. Brendon gets a beer for him and a glass of wine for me, and we warm up by the fire.

"I'm sorry we didn't get to finish the tour. I swear I had all this planned out. I just didn't think it was going to get that cold."

After taking a sip of wine, I lick my lips. "Don't be sorry at all! That was amazing and I learned so much."

He places his hand on top of mine. "Maybe we can just continue the tour on the next date?"

"I would love that."

Two glasses of wine later, I'm sufficiently warmed up enough to venture back out into the cold. It's weird, but I think I'm sad when Brendon is driving me home. I don't want our amazing date to end. When Brendon walks me to my door, I do get a kiss on my hand, which is incredibly sweet. We make sure to exchange phone numbers before he leaves.

The strangest part of the entire night is when I shut my eyes to go to sleep at night, I don't see Brendon—but I do see Nash.

❋ ❋ ❋ ❋ ❋

Saturday morning, I stumble into the kitchen to Mila making coffee.

"Bless your soul," I rejoice when she fills two mugs. After she hands one to me, we head to the couch and cuddle under a blanket. The first sip of coffee goes straight to my soul and I close my eyes to savor the moment.

"How was last night?" she asks over the rim of her mug.

"You know, it was pretty great. I haven't been on a good first date in a long time. It was nice and refreshing."

"So does that mean ..." Mila puckers her lips together and begins making smooching noises.

I giggle. "No. No goodnight kiss. He did kiss my hand, which is sweet in an old-fashioned kind of way."

"What was that?" Mila cups her free hand around her ear. "Did I just hear you say, 'Thank you, Mila. You were right'?"

"Thank you, Mila. You were right," I say through a laugh.

"You going to see him again, then?"

I bite my lip and nod. "I think so. Brendon was cute and fun. He took me on a walking tour downtown and showed me some of his favorite architecture. It was nice."

I watch her scan me up and down before my smile falters. "What's that look for?"

"No look."

"Yes, look. You have that all-knowing look. Did you talk to Trey?"

Mila sighs. "I just want you to be happy. If Brendon makes you happy, great. If Nash makes you happy, that's also great. I just don't want lines to get blurry, you know?"

I inhale sharply through my nose. "Here's the deal. Nash and I are strictly sex. Yes, we hang out together, but that's more to keep each other company. We already agreed that we aren't exclusive, so I don't feel bad for going on a date with Brendon. Nash is probably dating too."

She tilts her head. "But you don't know for sure?"

I shake my head, avoiding her judgmental gaze, and take a sip of my coffee.

"Are you going to tell Nash?"

I shrug my shoulders. "If it comes up, sure. But it doesn't matter, it's just—"

"Sex. Yeah, I heard you before. But just so you know, you never use the word 'nice' when referring to Nash."

I don't understand what Trey and Mila have against this whole friends-with-benefits thing. When the conversation is over, I bring up an even worse topic I've been avoiding.

"Susan won't stop calling me."

Mila straightens in her seat. "Why is your mother calling you?"

I shrug again. "Not sure. I keep ignoring her calls. So far, we're up to seven unanswered calls."

Mila chews her bottom lip before speaking again. "I'm not on your mother's side. You know that. But maybe you should answer. Maybe she has something new to say."

"What possibly could she have to say to me after all these years?" I snap.

Mila takes a calming breath. "I don't know, Tater Tot. I'm just saying that maybe, in the holiday spirit, you could answer. Isn't that what Jules would want?"

Jules. Her name sends shivers down my spine. I haven't even visited her yet this Christmas, like the horrible person I am.

Mila knows what hearing her name does to me. I can't believe she would ever use Jules's name when talking about my mom.

"I have to shower," I say flatly, standing up and walking away before Mila can say another word.

I wouldn't say things are necessarily awkward between Mila and me after that, but we have been somewhat avoiding each other for the past six hours. I've been watching Netflix in my room while Mila's been watching Hulu in the living room. It feels weird to be separated like this. I know she didn't mean to hurt me when she brought up Jules, but she knows that it's always hard for me to hear that name, let alone around Christmas.

Nash texted me a while ago, wanting to get drinks. He said he's picking me up soon and I suppose that means I should get out of bed and get ready. He's a nice guy, but I don't think even he would want to take me out in my current state. Greasy hair, a face that desperately needs to be washed, pajamas that probably should be in the hamper, and breath you could smell a mile away. Forcing myself out of bed, I brush my teeth (twice) and tame my hair with some dry shampoo. When I make it to my closet, all I want is my best friend to stumble into my room uninvited and give me her strong opinions.

"I need help!" I whine in the most dramatic way possible. The television turns off as Mila darts to my room.

"Are you okay?" she pants. A guilty smile crosses my face. I didn't think she would take me seriously.

"I don't know what to wear tonight."

Mila's concerned look turns to amusement as she shakes her head. "You are unbelievably annoying."

"And you are absurd. Now help me," I plead.

We both stare at each other for the briefest of moments before wrapping our arms tightly around one another.

"I'm so sorry. I should never have said that thing about Jules. It was totally out of line," she mumbles into my shoulder.

"You're not allowed to apologize. I'm the one who is supposed to apologize!"

Pulling back, I look into Mila's sad eyes. "You were right. I was just being stubborn. I am so sorry I acted like a jerk. Even though it's been so long, it's just still hard to hear her name, you know?"

Mila nods sympathetically. "Have you been to visit her this year?" When I shake my head, she continues, "Would you like some company? How long before Nash picks you up? We could go for a quick drive."

Nash's face pops into my head. I really want to see him, but I want to see Jules more. I've been too caught up in my own life. It isn't fair I haven't visited.

A smile forms on my face at the same time a tear rolls down it. I wipe it away, nodding frantically. Mila heads to her room to change and I send Nash a quick text.

T: Can I meet you at Tipsy? Mila and I have to run a super-quick errand before.

N: Sure! But as penance, I would love it if you wore your tight skinny jeans. Just a suggestion...

I softly laugh as I grab the jeans he's referring to from my closet.

I squint when we walk out into the sun and try sidestepping the patches of melting snow. Mila drives and neither of us speaks. There are no words. By the time we reach the cemetery, the sky has filled with gray clouds.

"You want me to come with you?" Mila asks as we sit in her parked car. I've never liked coming to a cemetery. I mean, who does? But I do it for Jules. I know she's always with me, but it feels different having a designated place to come to and talk to her. Remember her. I shake my head and open the door, the chilly air already stinging my face. Pulling my coat tighter around my body, I walk over and crouch in front of the stone I have become so familiar with over time.

"Hey, baby sister," I whisper, my fingers skimming over the words.

Taken too soon, but never forgotten. I will always love you, baby sister.
April 7, 1994-January 21, 2009.

My eyes gloss over as I stare at the picture of Jules and me at the beach that's set in the corner of her tombstone. We are both smiling from ear to ear, her in a flowy yellow striped sundress, me in jean cutoffs and a baggy tank top. I'm wrapping my arms around her neck from behind and, if I remember correctly, I think we were laughing at some guy who tried to hit on us. I looked ridiculous and asked to retake the picture, but Jules refused. She said the picture captured our essence. It was the most perfect day. My parents, being the absent people they were, didn't come with us. I only invited them on the trip because Jules begged me to. She always gave Mom and Dad more slack when it came to their parenting style. She and I spent the week at the Outer Banks in North Carolina, lying on the beach, swimming in the ocean, searching the sand for unique seashells, and just laughing together. It is one of my favorite memories of the two of us.

It probably isn't the most appropriate picture for a tombstone, but it was one of her favorites.

Her funeral was on a Tuesday. I wanted her at peace as soon as possible. Not trusting my parents, I planned the entire day myself down to what Jules wore— her favorite light blue off-the-shoulder flowy dress. I remember the day, but it's like it all happened in slow motion. The room was filled with family members, Jules's friends, and even some of her teachers. My parents seemed to treat the funeral like it was a social event and to this day I don't know if that was their way of coping or something else. The words 'I'm sorry for your loss' had zero meaning to me by the end of the day. It was weird; I would go through these moments when I couldn't breathe because I was crying so hard to laughing at some anecdote one of her friends shared with me. Towards the end of the day, some estranged relative approached me. She asked me if I knew about the white feathers. Super confused, I shook my head. She proceeded to tell me that when a loved one gets to heaven, they send down a white feather from their wings. They do this because they want to let you know they are at peace and happy and you should be too. Three days after Jules was laid to rest and I finally had the courage to enter her room, I found a white feather on her bed. It was the first time I genuinely smiled since she died.

My fingers pick up a white feather lying on the ground next to me now and the tears begin to fall before I even register what's happening. I look up at the sky, wondering if she's watching me right now.

"I miss you so much. You probably already know this, but it's Christmas time. I've been hanging out with this guy who happily indulges in my holiday craziness. You would like him. He took me to this Christmas-themed bar that had all these funny drink names. I swear we stepped right into the North Pole. You would've loved it." I laugh, but my heart isn't in it. "Mom keeps trying to call me. I can never bring myself to answer the phone. I wish you were here, baby sister."

This time, I'm not just tearing up. I'm full-on ugly crying. I shouldn't have even bothered to put on makeup.

"I love you so much," I mutter between sobs. When I feel a hand on my shoulder, I jump up and turn around, wrapping my arms around Mila's neck.

"Shh, it's okay," she whispers, rubbing my back.

I cry into her neck for what feels like hours. I finally stop when I feel physically and emotionally drained, my face frozen from the cold air. With an arm around my shoulders, Mila guides me back to the car. It takes some time for my breathing to return to normal and I wince when I remember I'm supposed to meet Nash.

> T: I am so sorry. I have to cancel. Do you work tomorrow? I still want to meet up. I promise this is not me backing out of our deal.

> N: Tomorrow sounds perfect. I have an idea that I think you will love.

Fourteen

Nash picks me up Sunday night and I make sure to wear the skinny jeans he loves. He meets me outside his car and I run to him, jumping into his arms. We laugh as he spins me around, brushing his lips against my cheeks. As I look into his eyes, my conversations with Mila and Trey echo through my head. On one hand, I guess I can understand why they would be nervous about feelings getting involved. But on the other hand, is it so wrong that I like the attention without all the extra strings of a relationship?

After thirty minutes of driving, I have no idea where we are.

Nash pulls into a parking lot and offers to help me out of the car. I tug my gloves on before interlacing our fingers together. Nash guides me up a cement path and sparkling lights fill my vision when we get to the top of the hill. A bright red sign reads 'Murrayville Light Show'.

"They're supposed to have the best lights in the county," Nash whispers in my ear as I jump in excitement.

Running ahead, I pay for our tickets and get a swift slap on my behind for it.

"This was supposed to be my treat," Nash says as he pushes his lower lip out.

"I know a way you could make it up to me." I wink in the most ridiculous way possible and Nash brushes his lips against mine, his hands sliding down to grab my ass. A clearing of a throat has us breaking apart.

Walking hand in hand, we follow the winding path through the most elaborate Christmas light displays I have ever seen. So far, my favorite is Santa Claus riding a polar bear. We're only halfway through the display when the first snowflake falls.

Stopping abruptly, I look up at the night sky. "This is my favorite kind of snow."

"I hate to break it to you, sweetheart, but there's only one kind of snow," Nash mocks.

I roll my eyes at him. "That's not true at all. The big chunky flakes that steadily fall throughout the day are, hands down, the best. Especially if you're watching them from inside. Then it looks like you're in a snow globe. The worst is when the super-small flakes combine with wind and whip you in the face the second you get outside."

Nash's mouth drops open and I give him a confused look.

"What?"

"Did the jolliest person in the world just admit they hate certain types of snow?" Nash places his hand on his chest as if I've offended him. "Santa's going to have to place you on the Naughty List."

"That is not what I said. I was simply stating what's the best snow and the worst snow. I never used the H-word. And don't even joke about that. I've worked very hard for my spot on the Nice List."

A low chuckle rumbles from his chest when he pulls me closer, placing one hand around my waist while grabbing my hand with the other.

"What are you doing?" I ask as I place my free hand on his shoulder. We begin to sway back and forth to the classical version of "Winter Wonderland" as the snow continues to fall.

"I just wanted to dance with a beautiful girl in the snow," he murmurs in my ear before twirling me. I yelp when he dips me, not expecting it, but he silences me with a soft and gentle kiss. A couple nearby begins to clap and we smile shyly before continuing our way through the lights.

As much as I hated rescheduling, I'm kind of glad I did. Due to it being a Sunday evening, most people are in their homes, getting ready for their work week. Other than a few people, Nash and I practically have the display to ourselves. It's perfect because we can take our time admiring the lights we love most while taking goofy pictures of each other at the same time.

"Want a pretzel?" Nash asks, nodding to the stand up ahead.

I nod with a smile and he pulls me along.

Placing the first bite into my mouth, I suck in a harsh breath.

"It was hot, huh?" Nash teases and I hip check him, grabbing another piece, this one a much better temperature.

"I've been meaning to ask you something," I blurt out as we continue walking.

"All right."

"Um, are we friends?"

Nash stops moving and I step in front of him. "Because I feel like we're friends," I continue. "I know we had a horrible first date and a weird start to whatever this is, but the more we hang out and have amazing sex, it feels like friendship. Is that stupid?"

When Nash doesn't answer immediately, my eyes widen and I feel the sweat start to form in my hairline even though it's beyond cold outside. I try to walk away, preserving whatever dignity I have left, but Nash grabs my elbow.

"Of course we're friends, you weirdo. I don't slow dance in the snow with just anyone." His smile makes me relax, even though I know he's about to make fun of me. I breathe a sigh of relief.

"So." He clears his throat, grabbing a loose tendril of my hair and twirling it around his finger. "Amazing sex, huh?"

I groan before swatting his chest and walking away. When he catches up to me, his hands wrap around my waist from behind and he presses a kiss to my temple.

Thankfully the light show is over shortly after we finish our pretzel. Don't get me wrong, the show was breathtaking, but the weather is turning frigid. I snuggle closer to Nash, trying to steal his warmth for my own selfish need. I don't think he minds. The snow hasn't let up and a fresh layer of white covers the path back to Nash's car.

"You know what I haven't done in the longest time?" Nash says, letting go of my waist.

"Huh?" I ask, glancing up towards the sky.

"Snowball fight!" he yells just as I feel the cold hit my shoulder.

I spin to look at him, my mouth dropping open. "I know you did not just hit me with a snowball."

He shrugs while making another. "I think I saw some hoodlums walk past. Want me to go beat them up?"

I shriek when another wad of snow flies at me and I successfully dodge it.

"Oh, it's on now."

Crouching, I mold the biggest snowball I can fit into my hands. When I glance up, Nash is busy making his own. I use the opportunity to hit him square in the chest. He acts as if he's been shot, which causes me to laugh and the distraction gets me a snowball to the leg. We both pick up our speed, blindly throwing snow back and forth. Tears stream down my face from laughter as I reach for more snow. When I spin around again, I find Nash bent over. Yelling like a crazy person, I run full speed at him, jumping on his back and smashing the snowball over his black beanie. He falls to his knees before dropping into the snow and I roll on top of him.

Quickly making another snowball, I hold it over his head. "Do you admit defeat?"

His chest vibrates with laughter as he holds his hands up. I drop the snow but don't notice when his right hand begins to move. Suddenly snow is smashed onto my hat, falling onto my face as Nash and I continue laughing. I fall beside him in the snow with the biggest smile on my face. Trying to catch my breath, I close my eyes and inhale the fresh smell of the snow.

"I haven't laughed that much in I don't know how long," Nash pants and I agree.

"I think my ass is now permanently frozen."

We turn to look at each other and start giggling all over again.

When both of us are officially icicles, we make our way back to the car and blast the heat as high as possible. Thankfully Nash has heated seats and I can feel my bottom again within minutes. Nash pauses with his hand on the gear shift and directs his attention to me. His eyes scan down my body and even though I'm fully decked out in winter gear, I feel as if he can see me. The real me. It's a surprising and strange feeling.

"Your place or mine?"

Somehow, we miraculously don't hit any red lights on the way home. Maybe that's fate's way of telling me tonight is going to be a good night. We head into Nash's building, waving a quick hello to Jeeves while rushing to the elevator. After we step in, Nash swipes his badge for the penthouse. We make it to the fourth floor before he presses the emergency stop button. His hands wrap around my waist, pulling my back to his chest.

He brushes my hair behind my shoulder. "You want to know the only downside about us hanging out in public?"

"What's that?" I ask, pulling my bottom lip between my teeth.

"That I can't do this to you."

His hand dips below my waistband and cups me, groaning into my ear all the while.

"No, we definitely can't do that in public," I tease through shaky breaths.

Eager and impatient, I move my hips as my head falls back on his shoulder. His breath is hot on my neck as he sucks on that sensitive spot behind my ear.

Nash twists my body around and backs me up against the wall. His lips find mine while his hands pin my wrists above my head. His hips hold me in place as his tongue meets mine. A gasp escapes my lips when I feel him press against my thigh and I weigh the pros and cons of having sex with him in the elevator. When I struggle to break free, he lets go of my wrists. His fingers dig into my hips as I push his jacket off his shoulders and unbutton his shirt.

"You swiped your key," I pant. "Does this elevator make any other stops when you do that?"

He shakes his head in response.

"Think you can make me come before we reach the top floor?"

He growls a warning and I shimmy around him, pushing the emergency button back to its original spot. The elevator springs to life and I brace myself on the railing. Nash pushes me into the corner, hovering over me.

"There are cameras in here," he informs me, "and I want to be the only one who sees you fall apart."

Five.

A shiver rushes down my spine as his hand slides down my pants, flicking my panties to the side.

His fingers barely touch me and I buck my hips as he toys with me. "Nash, please."

Six.

Two fingers are thrust inside me and Nash covers my mouth with his to silence me. He makes a come-hither motion with his fingers and my legs forget how to work, forcing me to hang on to Nash for dear life.

Seven.

Nash's eyes flutter shut when I reach down, rubbing his hard length through his pants. I attempt to undo the button on his jeans one-handed but fail miserably. Nash chuckles as he increases his speed.

Eight.

His breath tickles my ear as he whispers, "This isn't about me. I want to make you feel good. Come for me, Tatum."

Nash's thumb circles my clit before gently pinching it between his thumb and forefinger.

Nine.

Tossing my head forward, I moan into Nash's chest. Every single nerve-ending in my body is on fire and I come undone with Nash's name on my lips. He rides out my orgasm, peppering my neck with kisses.

Ten.

Nash runs his nose up the side of my jaw. "You look so incredibly beautiful when you come."

His lips capture my bottom lip and, using both hands this time, I successfully unbutton his jeans and pull down his zipper.

Eleven.

Reaching into his boxer briefs, I wrap my fingers around him, rubbing my thumb over the tip.

"I need this. I need you."

Twelve.

When we hear that final ding, I jump into Nash's arms. He kicks the coat I took off him into the apartment as he holds on tight to me. Being pressed against his chest is fantastic, but I desperately would rather do it with no clothes on.

"Shit!" Nash groans and I look down to see he walked us directly into the coffee table.

"You okay?"

"Yeah, I just didn't want to step on the cat. Go to your bed, Smelly."

I wave to Smelly Cat as Nash bites my earlobe. I never thought it would be hot to have a guy nibble on my ear, but I was wrong. So very wrong.

"Bedroom," I mumble in between kisses and he does as I say. When he tosses me onto his bed, we both strip as fast as humanly possible.

Nash hooks his hand under my thighs and twists me over in one fluid motion. Instinctively, I push my bottom closer to him and gasp in surprise when I feel his teeth nip at my exposed flesh. His hand skims up my spine, wrapping around the back of my neck. My fingers twist into the sheets as his hand slips between my legs.

"Watching you in the elevator was probably the hottest thing I've ever seen," he tells me as his fingers slide in and out of me.

"More," I plead.

"More?"

I nod into the pillow. Turning my head to face him, I say, "I need you inside me."

The bed dips when Nash kneels behind me, grabbing my hips and helping me onto all fours. He teases my entrance before filling me.

"Tatum," he breathes, leaning forward and palming my breast.

A sound I make only when I'm with him escapes my lips and I hear his smile in his evil laugh. Our bodies move together as the bed creaks beneath us. His fingers tangle in my hair as I arch my back into him.

Nash mumbles something unintelligible before increasing his pace. My vision blurs and I can't think straight. The squeaking of the bed frame gets louder with each thrust. Nash wraps his hand around my neck, guiding me back towards him. The position change causes us both to explode as he buries his face into my neck, his teeth grazing my skin. Our chests continue heaving up and down—then we hear a loud THUD. The next thing I know, Nash and I are falling off his bed and onto the floor. When I look up to see what happened, his bed frame is completely destroyed. We both burst out laughing, grabbing the comforter that is now on the floor and cuddling beneath it.

"I can definitely say that I have never broken a bed before." My head rests on Nash's chest as his arm drapes over my back, fingertips running up and down my spine.

"First for both of us, I guess," he laughs.

Reaching up, I place a small peck on his open lips. "A good first, friend."

His body tenses a little as I snuggle back into him.

We don't stay in our makeshift cocoon for much longer before getting up. I go to pick up my clothes only to find my jeans still damp from snow. When I frown, Nash hands me a pair of his sweatpants.

"You know, next time I go shopping I think I'm just going to have to buy double of my outfits if you keep stealing them all."

"Well, maybe if you didn't have such comfortable clothes, we wouldn't have this problem."

I stick my tongue out as I step into the soft fabric.

Nash bites his lower lip as he watches me. "The problem could also be solved by you just staying here."

My smile instantly falls and I look to see if he's serious. "I can't do that."

"Sure you can. If you wanted to." His tone is so casual that I can't tell if he wants me to stay for a matter of convenience for something else.

"Nash," I stutter, "we made our rules for a reason. Anyway, I have to get up early tomorrow. Thanks for the invite though."

Nash shrugs like it's no big deal and we both finish getting dressed.

When Nash grabs his keys, I place my hands on my hips. "What do you think you're doing?"

He glances at the keys and back to me. "Taking you home."

I shake my head. "That's sweet, but you should stay here and relax."

Nash approaches me, putting his hands around my waist. "I really don't mind driving you."

"And I really don't mind calling a car," I say with a smile.

I can tell Nash is fighting a smile. "Fine. But if I can't drive you, I'm at least paying for said car."

Walking around me, Nash goes to grab his phone.

"I can pay for my own car!"

Nash cups his hand around his ear. "What? I can't hear you. It's almost like you're out the door and getting in the car already."

Rolling my eyes, I laugh to myself. When the elevator arrives, I enter and sag against the wall after pressing the button for the lobby. I feel my phone vibrate and pull it out, somehow hoping it's Nash. That's crazy, though, because I haven't even been gone for five minutes. A weight forms in my stomach when I see Brendon's name.

> B: Haven't been able to stop thinking about you since our freezing cold walking tour. I hope you have officially warmed up since. Can I take you out again? I promise it will be an indoor activity.

I chew on my lip, a nervous habit I've tried to quit many times. This feels strange, leaving Nash's house and getting a text from another guy. I know Nash and I agreed we weren't exclusive, but it's still unnerving. I kind of feel dirty and not in a good way, but that isn't Brendon's fault.

> T: I loved our walking tour and am happy to report I have completely thawed out. I would love to go out again. What's your schedule like?

Brendon and I have been texting on and off since Sunday night, patiently waiting for our next date. Trey has been constantly rolling his eyes at me when he sees not only Brendon's name scroll across my phone but Nash's too. I don't know how many times I can explain to him that this was his girlfriend's idea. Mila was the one who decided four was the lucky number. He needs to save his eye rolls for her.

Fifteen

I haven't been able to stop thinking about Nash asking me to stay last night. It's not the first time and it probably won't be the last. He shrugged off my answer, but there was something in his eyes that made me think he was actually upset. I shouldn't care. I shouldn't be sitting at my computer obsessing over our situation instead of working or writing, but here I am.

Pinching the bridge between my nose, I inhale deeply and choose to focus on something other than my love life. I just need a good ending. One that makes my heart explode with joy. That's simple. Closing my eyes and leaning back in my chair, I imagine the two main characters in my novel. I can see them walking towards each other, her nervously pulling on the hem of her shirt and him with his hands stuffed deep into his pockets. They finally meet and he opens his mouth to say—

I clutch my chest as my heart plummets into my stomach at the loud phone ring filling the room. I look at my phone and sigh when I see it's just a text from Mila.

> M: Trey took me to work and I'm doing inventory all day so I won't be home till late. Save some dinner for me! And don't destroy my car!

I scowl, refusing to acknowledge the comment about her car. I have never hurt her precious baby and never would.

> T: In that case, I'm making chicken and vegetables, heavy on the vegetables.

> M: You're an evil woman.

Chuckling to myself, I click my phone shut and redirect my attention to my laptop. My eyes scan over the words I've now read at least a dozen times today. Biting on my lower lip, it dawns on me that I'm … upset. Upset that the text was from Mila and not Nash.

This was supposed to be just sex, no emotions. But what if I've hurt his feelings? As ridiculous as it is, Nash and I are probably the most stable thing in my life right now, and as weird as our situation is, I'm not ready to let it go.

Closing my laptop and coming to the realization that nothing is going to be written today, I head upstairs. After a quick shower, I spend minimal time applying some natural-looking makeup and curling my hair. Staring at my closet, I debate how to remedy this situation. I could just wear his clothes over with nothing underneath or …

When I finish getting dressed, I slide my feet into a pair of Mila's four-inch black leather heels and secure my trench coat around me. It's freezing out, so I run to the car as fast as I can in these heels. When I slide into the driver's seat, I grab a blanket from the back and lay it over my lower half. The entire drive to Nash's, I'm shaking in anticipation. Maybe I should've called him to make sure he was home first? No, it's more exciting this way. The second I park my car, my heart goes into overdrive.

With a polite smile, I wave to Jeeves as I pass him. His brow is furrowed in a question as he waves back, but I'm on a mission and don't have time to stop and ask him what's wrong. Stepping into the elevator, I take long, deep breaths. I've never done something like this before. It's more nerve-wracking than I thought it would be. I try to imagine what Nash's expression will be when he sees me. Shock? Horror? Oh God, please be the former.

When the doors open and I see no sign of Nash, I form a tight fist and rap my knuckles on the wall three times and wait. When I can't refrain from fidgeting, I stuff my hands in my coat pockets.

"Coming!" Nash hollers. The sound of his loafers on the hardwood floor gets louder with each step and I can hear my heartbeat.

Nash's brows knit together when he sees me. "Tatum?"

I wear my biggest smile and dart my tongue out just enough to tease him. "Miss me?"

Pushing past him, I grip the lapel of my coat.

"What are you doing here?" He chuckles.

Once the elevator doors close, I spin around and open my coat, placing my hands on my hips in a dramatic fashion.

His mouth falls open as he takes me in.

Swirling flowers embroidered on delicate black mesh that leaves absolutely nothing to the imagination cover my bra and panties. His eyes somehow grow even bigger when they take in my black garter belt with small gold clasps that hold up my thin black stockings.

Using my most seductive tone, I lower my voice and ask, "Now, what was your question?"

A growl is the only warning I get before Nash's body slams against mine, pushing me up against the wall and claiming my mouth. One hand cups my face possessively while the other fists around my curled hair and tugs, forcing my head back and exposing my neck. A moan escapes as I hook one leg around him, pulling his hips closer to mine. The hardness of him pressing against the small amount of material between us is almost too much for me to handle.

"Do you have any idea how sexy you are?" Nash mumbles as his lips move down my neck. His hand cups my breast before his teeth latch onto my nipple through the material. My body shakes, but Nash places a hand on my belly, holding me steady.

"I want to taste you. Tatum, would that be all right?" Nash asks with a coy smile.

I giggle. "Do you think I'm going to say no?"

Standing to his full height, his lips come back to mine, and Nash groans as our tongues meet again. Shrugging out of my coat, I hold on to Nash as it falls to the ground. His hands explore my body, sliding down the back of my panties and grabbing my ass. He's about to slide down my body, hopefully to do what he asked, when the ding of the elevator echoes through the room.

"Nashie! I'm home!" a female voice sings loudly as the door opens.

Holy motherfu— Who the hell is that? Nash presses his body to mine, shielding me from the stranger who just walked in.

"What the hell?" I mouth to Nash.

"Ever heard of calling ahead?" he shouts as I stare at him in shock and horror.

"Ever heard of getting a room? The elevator literally opens into your living room," she says with a bite.

"Clara! Privacy!" Nash barks.

"Oh, little brother. Relax. I have to go to the bathroom anyway."

"Little brother?" I whisper, my face buried in his chest. I keep my eyes tightly shut until I hear her footsteps fade and the lock on the bathroom door click. Placing both my hands on Nash's chest, I shove him away, grab my coat, and wrap it around myself as fast as humanly possible.

I smack his chest and keep my voice low. "You seriously attacked me like that when you had company coming over?"

This is, hands down, the most embarrassing moment of my life. As I pinch the top of my coat together, I run for the door. Nash grabs my arm and refuses to let go, no matter how much I squirm.

"Let me go! I'm half-naked and your sister is in the bathroom!" I yell-whisper.

Nash sighs as he rolls his eyes. "I'm sorry! Just stay. Borrow more of my clothes."

"That is the absolute worst idea in the world. I—" Not letting me finish my statement, Nash drags me into his room, shutting the door behind us. After digging through his drawer, he tosses me a pair of joggers and an old T-shirt.

"Nash—"

"Please. Stay," he breathes before leaving me alone.

Never in my life have I had something like this happen to me! How can I possibly go back out there and face his sister with a straight face? How do I know she didn't see me practically naked before Nash's body covered mine? I groan in frustration and stamp my feet on the ground like a child. Taking a deep breath, I realize I have to walk back through the living room whether I decide to leave or not. Stripping my coat off and laying it on his bed, I dress in his clothes and pray this day can't get any worse. As I open the door, I remember I just have to breathe. Inhale through the nose, exhale through the mouth.

"There she is!" Clara beams before pulling me into a tight hug. Shocked by her gesture, I lightly pat her back while Nash gives me an awkward thumbs-up. When she releases me, she giggles. "I'm so sorry about what just happened. Nashie knew I was coming over, so I'm surprised he didn't warn me or tell Jeeves to have me wait."

Nash scrubs a hand down his face. "Obviously I forgot, and can you not call me that?"

She waves a hand dismissively at him and turns back to me. "He didn't tell me he was seeing someone either and he definitely forgot to mention that you are hot!"

A nervous smile spreads across my face as Nash pushes off the couch. "Leave her alone, Clara."

He grabs Clara's elbow and guides her away from me, then places a kiss on my cheek.

"Nashie can be a little touchy. Well, can you at least stay for lunch? I would love to learn about the woman who has stolen my brother's heart."

"Oh," I stutter, "I appreciate the invite, but—"

"Yes, stay," she says. "I ordered way too much Thai from that place down the street."

Chewing on my lip, a crease develops on my forehead.

Nash opens his mouth, but Clara speaks first. "Then it's settled. What can I get you to drink?"

"Oh, um, water would be fine."

"Vodka, it is!" Clara bounces off the couch and heads straight for the bar.

I lower my voice so only Nash can hear me. "Are, are you sure? I don't want to intrude more than I already have."

Nash takes a step closer to me. "You don't have to stay if you're uncomfortable, but I would love it if you did."

I nod as I intertwine our fingers. "She's not serious about the vodka, right? It's only noon."

He shrugs like this is normal behavior for her.

Our food arrives just as Clara is setting a tray of drinks on the coffee table. I grab mine and smile as I bring it to my lips. Holy crap, that's strong. I quickly decide that I will be only taking the tiniest of sips, and only when she's looking.

Nash is paying the delivery man as Clara moves closer to me. "So, how did you meet my little brother?"

I almost say a dating app, but then change my mind. Nash might not have told his sister and I would hate to reveal his secrets that way. "I cut my hand on some glass and he was my doctor."

Her hands cover her mouth. "Oh, my gosh! That is the cutest thing ever!"

My smile spreads as I remember that it was the opposite.

"Actually," I clear my throat and look over at Nash, "it wasn't. The first time we met, we couldn't stand each other."

Crossing her legs, she tilts her head. "So what changed?"

"Well ..."

How can I answer this simply? Probably telling her that we started sleeping together would be too much information. "You know, I'm not exactly sure what happened. It just kind of changed."

She must be content with my answer because she stands up with her drink and walks over to the kitchen to help Nash unpack the food.

Is this weird? Me staying for lunch with his sister? Isn't meeting the family what girlfriends do, not friends with benefits? Or maybe it's weird that this doesn't feel weird. Clara is nice and I'm surprised that I want to stay. And that Nash wants me to stay.

Nash's eyes connect with mine and he gestures with his head for me to join them; I conveniently forget my drink. I sit down next to Clara at his glass dining table and Nash hands me a plate overflowing with food.

"Clara, do you live close by, then, or is this a special visit?" I ask.

Clara swallows the bite of food in her mouth before answering. "I'm heading out of town for a while and just wanted to see little Nashie before I left."

Ignoring Nash's frown when he stands up and walks to the sink, "Where are you going?"

"Bahamas. My boyfriend and I won the lottery a while back and the Bahamas has been on my bucket list forever."

My eyebrows shoot into my hairline. "Wow! That's amazing. The Bahamas and the lottery."

Nash returns with a glass of water for me and I mouth, "Thank you."

She giggles, then looks at Nash, then at me. "So. I need some gossip."

"No! No! No!" Nash waves his hands in front of his face.

"You know," I say as I try to think about anything Nash has done that would be classified as embarrassing. "I honestly can't think of anything. Usually, I'm the one making a fool of myself."

"I wouldn't say that," Nash mumbles while making some intense eye contact with me.

When I smile back, Clara asks, "Do I need to go to the bathroom again?"

I laugh, covering my mouth so I don't spit food everywhere. "God, no! But you can tell me what Nash was like as a kid."

Clara rubs her hands together looking somewhat like an evil queen. "Did he tell you about how he used to play doctor with my stuffed animals and Barbies?"

"What?" I bark out a laugh.

She nods with the biggest grin. "I'd always be looking for my toys and I'd find him listening to their hearts with his toy stethoscope or testing their reflexes with the little mallet thing."

Nash groans, "A reflex hammer. You mean a reflex hammer."

"Yeah, whatever." She tosses her blond hair over her shoulder. "He would even write down random numbers on a notepad and when I asked him what he was doing, he told me he had to take their numbers down so they didn't die."

"Vitals," he whines. "I said vitals. Can we change topics? Please?"

"Of course not! I have so many more stories and have never had anyone to share them with before!" Clara reaches over and grabs my hand. "Give me your number and I can send you some baby pictures of Nash. He loved to take off his diaper, place it on his head, and run around the house screaming 'Look at my wee-wee.'"

"That's it." Nash pushes back from the table, gestures for Clara to get up, and has her sit back down in a chair far away from me.

The rest of lunch is spent laughing, mostly at Nash's expense. When he disappears for a moment, Clara takes advantage and we swap phone numbers in secret. She's kind of incredible. Part of me is envious of Nash and I think it's because I miss this. Laughing and talking about nothing and everything with family. The other part of me is excited I was able to meet Clara and learn more about this amazing guy I'm ... friends with. Just friends with.

Once my entire plate is empty, I get the feeling that I am interfering and need to make a timely exit.

After finishing my glass of water, I announce, "Thank you so much for inviting me for lunch, but I really should let you two have some sibling time."

"You're leaving already?" Clara asks with a slight pout.

I nod. "I should get back home and do some actual work anyway."

"I'll walk you out," Nash says. His hand slips under the hem of my shirt, finding the dip in my lower back.

Just as I'm about to press the button for the elevator, Nash steps in front of me and cups my face in his hands. "I don't think I'll ever be able to apologize enough. I had no idea you were coming over or I would've warned you."

I chuckle. "It's okay. You can repay me by just never talking about this again."

He cocks his head to the side, looking as if I've offended him. "Hell, no! You can't wear something like that," he gestures to my body, "and expect me to never talk about it again. Do you know how goddamn edible you looked?"

Nash's lips find my neck and I giggle as I wrap my arms around him.

"Here's the game plan," he mumbles into my skin. "I'm going to get Clara to leave as soon as possible and when I do, I'm coming over to your place and you'd better still be wearing—"

I lean away from him and cover his mouth with my hand. "We're not talking about it again! And as amazing as that sounds, you should have some family time. I'm so sorry I interrupted it. I just thought ..."

I trail off, wishing I hadn't said anything.

Nash frowns. "You just thought what?"

I shrug. "You just seemed kind of bummed last night when I left, and then when I didn't hear from you this morning, I just assumed you were mad at me."

Nash rubs the back of his neck while shaking his head.

"What?"

He smiles. "You're crazy, you know that? I didn't text you because I got called in last night and was sleeping all morning. I was just about to reply when you showed up at my door. You do know that the phone works both ways, right?"

I roll my eyes, push him out of the way, and press the elevator button.

"I'm just saying." I love how he smiles when he laughs.

I turn around to meet his smug grin. "Okay, fine. Maybe I was overanalyzing the situation." When his smugness doesn't fade, I say,

"I promise I will never overanalyze again and that means I'll never do anything like wear skimpy lingerie to your house ever again."

"Now wait a second—"

When the elevator doors open, I jump in so he can't grab me.

"Bye-bye!" I wave and blow a kiss. When the doors shut, I collapse against them.

What just happened?

Sixteen

Later that night, I spread out on the couch and am scrolling through channels when a chips-and-dip commercial comes on. Damn, those chips look crispy. I guess since Mila is still at work and I happen to be wearing a bra, it must be fate.

After said chips and dip are acquired, I hurry back to the car. It might seem a little sad that I am so excited about my purchase, but unfortunately, that's what life is like when you're over twenty-five. Mila has always been super generous with lending me her car, so I make sure to drive slowly and triple-check before I pull out of the store parking lot. Following a large red truck, I keep my right hand on the steering wheel while my left tangles in my hair.

I must be hungry because I start thinking about how delicious the chips are going to taste. Maybe I'll eat them in bed. While I watch some trashy show. I bet Nash would eat chips in bed with me. Wait—

My eyes widen in fear as a random object appears in the road. I grab the steering wheel with both hands and slam my foot down on the brake, only to hit it head-on.

When the car stops, I shut my eyes and whisper, "Oh, my God! Please don't be an animal. Please don't be an animal."

Since no one else is on the road, I put my hazard lights on and step out of the car. Slowly creeping around to the front, I blink a few times to make sure what I'm seeing is actually what I'm seeing.

"You have to be joking."

Lying on the ground and slightly under the car is a fan. A freaking fan! Why the hell is there a fan in the middle of the road!? I pick up the very mangled appliance and closely examine it. It's small, like something you would keep in the corner of your room on your dresser. I look around, still extremely confused. There's no way anyone is going to believe this happened. Mila is going to kill me.

The front of the car doesn't seem to be damaged. I kneel down and peer under the car with the flashlight on my phone. I don't see anything, but I don't really know what I should be looking for. Taking a deep breath, I grab my phone and do what I have to do.

Where the hell is Mila? I thought she was only doing inventory. She should have her phone on her! I call her three times and Trey twice and get tired of leaving anguished voicemails telling them to call me back. Chewing on my lip, only one other name flashes through my mind. Before I can think too much about why that name appeared, I press dial.

"I need your help."

Nash clears his throat. "Are you okay?"

"I'm fine, but I'm not sure about Mila's car. Can you come get me? I haven't seen any cars drive by and I'm stranded somewhere on Seventh Street."

Fifteen minutes later, a shiny black Lexus stops behind Mila's car, and my lips part when Nash steps out. He's wearing a button-down shirt with the sleeves rolled up to his elbows, looking unbelievably delicious. In my mind, he's running in slow motion to save me, channeling his inner "Baywatch." My mouth turns dry as I picture Nash unbuttoning his shirt, tossing it to the ground, and—after verifying my safety—taking me on the hood of Mila's car, not caring that anyone could drive past and see. My fantasy is ruined the second he opens his mouth.

"What did you do?" he asks.

"Where's your coat?" It's freezing out and he doesn't look at all bothered by the cold.

"I'm warm-blooded. Now, what did you do?"

My hands find my hips, insulted he just assumed it was my fault. "What makes you think I did something? What if the car just randomly stopped working?"

He gives me a look that conveys he knows I'm full of shit. "And did the car just stop working?"

"Not exactly." I sigh, my shoulder drooping. "I ran over a fan."

Nash's brows pull together as he leans closer. "I'm sorry, what did you say?"

"A fan. I ran over a fan."

My irritation grows when Nash doesn't respond. He just continues to stare at me like I said something to him in Japanese.

"Nash!"

"Please explain to me how one runs over a fan. Was it like a ceiling fan?"

I roll my eyes. "No. Like one of those small oscillating fans you put on your desk. The truck in front of me cleared it, but Mila's car is way lower to the ground so I didn't see it."

"And you ran over a fan," he says the words slowly as if he still isn't comprehending the situation.

"Yes! I ran over a fan! Now, tell me what to do."

"How would I know what to do?"

I shrug. "I don't know. You're a guy. Aren't all guys supposed to know about car stuff?"

He holds up a finger. "I will definitely make fun of you for that comment later, but right now I'm still trying to process what is happening."

"I really wanted some chips and dip."

When I pause for too long, he says, "Is that the end of the story? Because that explains nothing. How did you get from chips and dip to killing a fan?"

I hang my head in embarrassment. "So I went to the store and on my way back I—"

"Ran over a fan. Yeah, you said that." Nash looks around the road. "So where's the fan? Unless there isn't one. You know, you could have just said you missed me instead of making up this ridiculous story."

Walking to the backseat, I open the door and grab the object in question. A sheepish smile crosses my face as I hold it up for his viewing.

Nash's smile grows and he doubles over in laughter. "Only you, sweetheart."

After I toss the fan back into the car, I swat Nash on the shoulder.

"It's not funny," I say through small giggles.

"You're telling me you were driving down the road and ran over a fan and I'm not allowed to laugh?" He wipes a tear from the corner of his eye.

The laughter finally spills from my lips and we both are unable to control ourselves.

A solid five minutes later, when we both calm down, Nash cups my face with his hands.

His thumb strokes my jaw, sending shivers down my spine. "Are you okay? Did you get hurt or anything?"

I shake my head. "Not yet. I'm sure when I tell Mila what I did, she might murder me, though."

"We can't have that," he mumbles, pressing his lips to my cheek. He walks past me and my face falls when he opens the driver's side door.

"What the hell are you doing?" I practically scream.

He looks at me with a blank expression. "You said you needed help. I'm going to try to see if it's at least drivable."

I jump in front of him and push him back. Okay, I *try* to push him back but he doesn't move.

"Did you not just hear me? Mila. Murder. What if you drive it and make it worse somehow? What if it blows up and now not only have I destroyed Mila's car, but I killed the only guy who's been giving me orgasms lately?"

Laughing, Nash pulls out his phone and walks a few paces away. As I watch him, my fingers brush over the skin he just kissed. It was such a comforting gesture that makes me so happy I called him.

Are Mila and Trey right? Is this turning into more than just sex? It would explain why I was so determined to go to his house earlier today to prove he wasn't mad at me. Wait, no! That's crazy. This is just two adults who happen to be having phenomenal sex together, helping each other out. And obviously, he only asked if I was hurt because he's a doctor.

"My mechanic will be here soon," he informs me when he returns.

"You have your own mechanic? I didn't know you were that rich."

He chuckles. "The guy I use keeps his garage open late. He'll come out and take a look at the car. Let you know if there are any obvious signs something is wrong."

I let out a low breath. My phone starts to sing—'I kissed a girl and I liked it'—which results in a surprised look from Nash. I roll my eyes at the ringtone Mila assigned herself.

"It's Mila. Should I answer it?" I ask with a shaky voice.

He shakes his head. "I wouldn't. Let's talk to Sal before we worry her for nothing."

When Sal the mechanic pulls up in his tow truck, my eyes widen in fear.

"A tow truck? I thought you said we shouldn't worry yet," I nearly shout at Nash.

"It's probably just a precaution," he reassures before kissing me on my temple. Another sweet gesture.

When Sal walks over, he and Nash do some guy handshake and I smile politely.

"What do we have here?" Sal asks.

"I ran over a fan," I quietly say.

"Huh?"

I clear my throat. "I said, I ran over a fan."

Sal reacts the same way Nash did, and I'm forced to bite my tongue so I won't scream out of frustration. When Sal looks at Nash, Nash nods and shows him the fan.

"Well, um. That's a first. What happened?"

I explain what I told Nash about how it just appeared out of nowhere. Sal nods in understanding then lies on the ground under Mila's car. He grunts a few times, but says nothing that assures me I haven't destroyed my best friend's car.

What feels like hours later, Sal stands up and dusts off his hands.

"You're lucky. Car looks good. When Nash said you hit something, I expected damage."

I almost jump up and down from the good news. "Wait, seriously?"

Sal holds up a hand. "Now, I'm not saying the car is in perfect shape. That is just my opinion by a quick observation. I see the car is due for inspection soon, so if anything is wrong, wherever you take it will tell you. Until then, just keep your eyes peeled for any ... obstacles in the road."

Nash cracks up while I fake laugh.

"Thanks, Sal. I'm good to drive it home, then?"

Sal nods and then tips an invisible hat to Nash and me before getting back in his truck and driving off.

I throw my head back, truly breathing for the first time since I called Nash. "I just dodged the biggest bullet ever! Mila loves her car!"

"Seriously?" Nash looks at the peeling paint and salt stains.

I nod. "It's the car she lost her virginity in, and that has sentimental value to her."

Nash takes a step away from the car. "Right. Do you want me to follow you back? You know, just in case?"

I tilt my head to the side. "Just in case what?"

He shrugs, kicking a pebble at his foot. "I don't know. Maybe the car stops again and the only way to get it going is by you having sex in the backseat with an insanely sexy friend."

I laugh and shake my head. "You're an idiot."

As I'm climbing in the car, Nash props himself in the doorway, looking down at me through hooded eyes. "Are you still wearing the sexy bra and panties?"

I pull the door with extra force and watch him and his stupidly perfect smirk walk away.

Nash does in fact follow me home, and we may or may not have a quickie in the backseat of Mila's car. Nash also may discover I am in fact still wearing my sexy lingerie. For obvious reasons, Nash and I agree we will deny any events that took place tonight if ever questioned.

❄ ❄ ❄ ❄ ❄

Wednesday afternoon, I finish work, ignore another call from my mother, and get ready for my date with Brendon. One of the local movie theaters is having a screening of *Arthur Christmas* and I could not be more excited. Not only have I not seen that movie yet this year, but I've never seen it on the big screen. Pittsburgh is really upping its holiday spirit this year.

Brendon's finger is frozen in mid-air, about to ring the doorbell, when I open the door.

"Hey!"

His smile is sweet and genuine. "Hey, yourself."

When I hear Mila's shoes coming down the hall, I grab Brendon's arm and rush him to his car in hopes of avoiding my amazing best friend, her boo, and the interrogation that would follow. Brendon and I make polite conversation while he drives to the Riverside Movie Theater. I continually glance at his hand resting on his thigh and wonder why he hasn't tried to at least hint at holding hands. Maybe he's just not a touchy-feely kind of guy? Nash doesn't seem to mind touching my hand or my thigh or my —

"We're here."

I snap out of the thoughts I was having. I can't seriously be thinking about Nash right now.

After parking, we walk closely but not touching. Brendon pays for our tickets and I buy drinks and popcorn with the most disgusting shine of butter on it. Spoiler alert: it's delicious. The movie is adorable, even with toddlers screaming and fussing throughout the entire showing. Just as we're about to head back into the cold, I notice they sell ice cream at the concession stand. Brendon indulges me and we each get a scoop of cookies n' cream before finding a table off to the side.

"Thanks for bringing me here. Seeing the movie on a screen bigger than forty inches was pretty awesome," I say between bites.

Brendon chuckles. "I'm glad you had fun."

I suck the extra cream off my spoon while watching Brendon's eyes travel over me. Leaning forward on the table, I say, "Tell me something about yourself."

His eyebrows raise. "Something about me? Other than that I'm insanely handsome?"

"Obviously."

He chews on his lip as he thinks. "It's kind of deep. Are you ready for that?"

In a teasing fashion, I pretend to fasten a seat belt over my chest before bracing my hands on the table. This makes Brendon smile.

"I was married."

Wow. That is not at all what I thought he was going to say.

"Brinley and I dated for five years before we finally tied the knot. I'm not sure what happened, but once the rings went on our fingers things changed. I probably should have told you this before we went out, but legally I'm still married. We've been separated going on eight months now and have almost no contact. The divorce process is unbelievably slow, but we are getting divorced. I just think it's something you should know."

I clench my teeth to keep my jaw off the sticky ground. I'm dating a married man? How was this not in his profile? Better yet, why didn't he wait to make a profile until after he was officially divorced? Trying to process this in my head is clearly taking longer than he expected. His face is scrunched up and uncomfortable, like his ice cream has gone sour.

"Okay," is all I manage to say, but his facial expression doesn't change. I run my free hand over the back of my neck, not sure what I'm supposed to say or do next.

Brendon sighs. "I get it if you want to stop seeing me. The reason I told you was because I don't know if I'm ready for another relationship. I've had a blast spending time with you and I want to continue seeing you, but I don't think I want anything exclusive. Is that okay?"

Finally, I swallow the lump that has lodged itself in my throat. "Kind of see where life takes us?"

"Exactly!" His entire body relaxes into his seat and I nod.

After we finish our ice cream, we make our way back to the car. As I go to shove my hands in my pockets, Brendon interlaces our fingers and I cuddle into his side. He's cozy and warm, but not like Nash is. I've never been in this type of situation before, where I'm stuck comparing two guys. I don't want to. It's not fair to Brendon, but it's like Nash was a cloud hovering above us all night. Brendon says goodnight with another adorable kiss on my hand before heading back out into the snow. I enjoy Brendon's company, but I'm not sure if I can date someone who is legally still married. It just doesn't seem right. He said they have almost no contact, but what does that even mean? Maybe if my brain didn't short circuit when he told me, I could've asked.

Seventeen

"What's going on, Tater Tot?"

Mila sits in the chair opposite me. I only have ten minutes left in the workday and have finished all my assignments, so now I'm sitting at my desk and playing on my phone.

"Just waiting to clock out."

Mila is staring at me with the most awkward smile. She wants something, I'm just not sure what. She's practically dancing in her chair when I say, "Out with it."

"How was your date? I need all the juicy details!"

"Juicy details? You know our walls are extremely thin and I hear your juicy details all night. I don't think you need any more ideas."

She rolls her eyes and throws a wadded-up sticky note at me. "You're stalling. Now spill."

Sighing heavily, I know I have to tell her. Whether it's today or tomorrow, I can't keep something like this from her. Even if I tried, Mila is one person I could never hide anything from.

"It was, um, informative."

"Not exactly a word I would use to describe a date."

Inhaling sharply, I rip the Band-Aid off. "Brendon is married."

Mila was in the process of putting a piece of gum in her mouth and is now frozen mid-air. I lean across my desk and stuff the gum into her mouth before pushing her chin closed.

"Married? Isn't that something that should've been in the damned profile?" she shrieks.

"I know, right? He said they are getting divorced and he's just jumping on the dating train right away."

Mila leans back in her chair, eyes wide while she shakes her head back and forth.

"You okay?" I ask.

"That's just a lot of information to process. What did you do or say?"

I shrug. "We said we would continue hanging out and see where it goes. Who knows, maybe the next time we're out, we'll realize we're awful together."

"Uh-huh," she mumbles skeptically.

I wrinkle my forehead and point a finger at her. "Don't judge. You put me on these apps. This is the result."

She runs both hands through her hair. "Anything else crazy you want to tell me while my mind is still blown?"

Taking a deep breath, I quickly say, "I ran over a fan with your car and I think it's okay, but I'm not one-hundred percent sure. Also, Nash and I had sex in the backseat."

Squinting, she moves her chair closer to my desk. "What?"

I repeat myself at a normal speed.

"You ran over something with my car?" she yells.

"Yes. Let's focus on that. And it was a fan! It just appeared out of nowhere. I'm so sorry!" I plead.

Exhaling softly, she murmurs, "This is not at all the conversation I thought we were going to have when I came down here."

"I'm so sorry. Nash had a guy take a look at it and he said the outside looked fine and if something was wrong, it would be found when you get your car inspected."

The corners of her mouth begin to turn up. "Nash? Was he with you when this all happened? Oh, my God! Did you live out my mechanic-and-helpless-woman fantasy in my car?"

Mila is like a dog with a bone and I just provided her with a nice juicy one; no pun intended.

"Ew! No, I called him. You and Trey weren't answering your phones and I didn't know what to do. They don't teach you in Driver's Ed what to do when you run over a fan."

Mila's laughter is immediate and I just sit and wait. I've told this story so many times that I'm now immune to the humor.

"I mean, it's not like Nash's naked ass is the first one that backseat has seen."

A laugh bubbles in my throat.

Mila takes a deep breath to calm herself. "A fan? Like an actual fan?"

"Yes, a fan. I put its carcass out in the garage."

Mila jumps from her chair, running out the door. What now sounds like a cackle echoes through the house and I know that I will never live this down.

Friday night's dinner is brought to Nash and me by Golden House, which is only a few blocks away from Nash's penthouse. The amount of food we ordered could easily feed a family of eight, but we welcomed the challenge. After clearing off Nash's coffee table, I organized our Chinese takeout containers while Nash retrieved plates and silverware. The second Smelly Cat smelled food, she jumped up on my lap, purring up a storm.

"Wow, looks like I've been replaced," Nash teases when he approaches us.

"What are those for?" I nod towards the cutlery in his hands.

"Um, to eat with," he responds with a curious look as he sits down next to me.

"They gave us chopsticks," I inform him as I open a pair up and snap them apart.

"Well, at least use a plate." Nash tries shoving a plate onto my lap, pushing Smelly Cat off, but I refuse.

"Are you trying to tell me you'll have sex with me, but won't share a takeout container of food with me?"

Before he can get a chance to answer, I twirl a giant helping of noodles with my chopsticks and stuff it all into my mouth. Narrowing his eyes, Nash goes to snatch the container away when I plunge my used chopsticks back into the food. When a slight smile forms on his face, I cover my mouth and laugh.

We take turns picking at each dish, sometimes even sharing our food while *The Christmas Chronicles* plays in the background. I've already watched it three times this year, so it's easy to follow while I'm doing other things.

"What happened to your face?" I ask, causing Nash to choke on his rice.

"What's wrong with my face?"

I laugh. "I didn't mean your face. Sorry. I meant the little scar above your left eyebrow. How'd you get it?"

Nash narrows his eyes. "Way to keep a man humble. It's just stitches from my childhood. I was playing on the jungle gym with some friends and for some stupid reason they were throwing rocks up the slide and I was catching them. The day is a blur, but they claim they told me to move when I was telling them I was going home. Next thing I know, a rock is smashing into my face and I'm heading to the hospital."

"Ouch!" I wince, imagining the type of pain he went through.

He shrugs. "It's cool. Chicks dig scars, right?"

"You know." I take another bite of lo mein as I ignore his comment. "I've been meaning to ask you something."

"What now?" Nash pretends to be annoyed, but I see the smirk he's hiding.

"Why are you single?"

His fork stops mid-air for only a moment. "I believe that's listed under personal questions, which is against the rules."

I shake my head and swallow the wad of food in my mouth. "That's not what the rules say."

"It isn't?" His one eyebrow quirks up.

"Nope. The rules just state that you can't ask *me* questions. So, why are you single?"

Setting his fork down, Nash rubs the back of his neck as if I'm making him uncomfortable. Believe it or not, that's not my intention. For some reason, I just want to get to know the guy. I settle back in my seat on the leather couch and wait.

"I was engaged," he says slowly and I let that sink in. Holy shit! Nash was engaged? "Her name was Sassy—"

I unintentionally start choking on my veggies. "I'm sorry. Please tell me that's a joke." When he shakes his head, I add, "Was she a stripper?"

He chuckles at this. "Not a stripper. She was actually in my program at Brown."

"Of course, you went to Brown," I tease and Nash lightly smacks my leg.

"Sassy and I dated a long time and then I proposed. It's what you did in my family, you know? You went to college, found a suitable partner, dated, and got married, all while working towards the dream of becoming a doctor."

"How romantic," I deadpan. I place my chopsticks in my container, wanting to hear more. Needing to hear more. This is the first time I've ever asked Nash something so serious and gotten an answer. I like talking to him.

His fists open and close in frustration as his eyes narrow. Part of me regrets inadvertently bringing up his ex.

"I proposed to her in a super-obnoxious way. Sassy loved to be the center of attention and I almost feel like she would've said no if I didn't ask her in front of other people. Anyway, two days after we got engaged, I found out she was sleeping with one of my old college roommates."

Nash speeds through the last sentence before shoving more beef and broccoli into his mouth. My lips part and I'm frozen in horror. She cheated on him with his former roommate? What a cliché.

"Nash." I place my hand on his arm. "I am so sorry. How did you find out?"

He starts to laugh a little like a crazy person before running his free hand through his hair. "Oh, that was great. I forgot my badge for work and when I came back to get it, I found Sassy and Mark in bed together. Our bed. That we had just had sex in only a few hours prior. That was about a year ago."

I tighten my grip on his arm but he shrugs me off.

"Nash—"

"Want some? It's delicious." Nash asks and points to his container of food. Not wanting to push him, I lean forward, open my mouth and allow him to place the fork full of food on my tongue. He wasn't kidding; this is delicious. His thumb wipes some soy sauce from my lip. I go to hand him a napkin, but he brings his thumb to his mouth and sucks.

Does it make me an awful person that I want to know what the ring looked like? Does he still have the ring? I'm only curious because as I sit on a sofa that probably cost more than my entire house, I can only imagine the enormous rock Sassy sported for a total of forty-eight hours.

"Go ahead and ask," Nash says while staring me down.

"Ask what?" My fingers rub up and down Smelly Cat's spine, who is curled up in a ball next to me.

"About whatever is on your mind. I know you and I know you want to ask me something."

Damn, he's good. He has to have some mind-reading superpowers.

"Tell me I'm wrong."

I huddle further under the blanket. "What did the ring look like? I have to know!"

Nash chuckles before indulging me. "It was a plain white gold band, an oval diamond in the center surrounded by a cluster of small diamonds."

My jaw falls to the floor. "It sounds beautiful. What did you do with it?"

"Do with it when?"

"When you got it back from Sassy." My entire body shivers, saying her stupid name.

Nash clears his throat before taking a drink of water. He shakes his head before stuffing more food into his mouth. Why do I suddenly feel like he's avoiding the question? Oh. my God!

"You didn't get the ring back, did you? What you just described sounds insanely expensive and beautiful and you let the cheating bitch keep the ring? What's her address?"

Nash laughs quietly. "What? Are you going to head over and demand the ring back?"

"I might. She is the last person on this planet that should have that ring. Your ring."

"It's not my ring. I bought it for her."

Is he seriously trying to defend her?

"And she lost the privilege to keep it when she opened her legs for someone who wasn't her fiancé."

Nash mouths, "Wow!"

I take a breath and settle back into the cushions. "Okay. Maybe I'm a little heated. Obviously I won't go over to her house, but I just don't think that's fair. You bought a gorgeous engagement ring for her because you thought you two would be together forever. I just think it's not right."

"All right." Nash wipes off his hands with a napkin, rolls it into a ball, and tosses it on the table. "Your turn." I furrow my brow in question. "Screw the rules. Tit for tat. Why are you single?"

I clear my throat. "That's such a boring story. You don't want to sit here and listen—"

"Blah, blah, blah. Cough it up, Tate."

He's right. I just made him relive an awful memory out of pure curiosity. Carefully, I place my food on the coffee table and wipe the sweat from my hands on my jeans. It's been a while since I've talked about Johnny, even with Mila. I suppose it's time Nash knows what a true mess I am.

"Johnny Sutto." My eyes focus on the gray knitted blanket over our laps. "We dated for seven months. Everything seemed to happen so fast. We met and then a week later it had felt as if we'd known each other for years. Johnny and I started to date and everything was great. Until it wasn't."

"What does that mean?"

I finally look up to find that Nash has put his food down too, fully invested in my story. His eyebrows pinched together, his mouth a hard line.

Taking a deep breath, I slowly exhale. Not even Mila knows this part of the story. I always told her that things just fizzled out. I suspect she doesn't believe me, but she's never pushed the issue.

"When Johnny broke up with me, he said that I liked him too much." I close my eyes, not able to look at Nash. "We were, well, I guess I was making plans for the future. He said, um, he said he couldn't see a future with me and that I wasn't enough for him."

Truthfully, I'm not even hurt by Johnny's words anymore. If anything, I'm more embarrassed that I spent so much time with someone who thought so little of me. Now that I'm thinking of it, I don't think I've made any long-term plans since. Things fall apart too easily and it sucks getting your hopes up.

Silence fills the large living room and I can't bring myself to make eye contact with Nash. Instead, I choose to focus on my breathing. In and out. In and out. Finally, I summon all my courage and look up.

"Say something," I whisper.

"How the fuck aren't you enough? Has this Johnny asshole ever even talked to you?"

"Nash—"

"How is it possible for some guy to date you and not see how amazing you are? Not only are you the most beautiful girl I've ever seen, but you have the biggest heart. You are so unbelievably optimistic that it's painful sometimes. You love life more than anything and for this waste of space to tell you you're not enough, it's complete bullshit!"

His intense reaction surprises me. And his words make my heart ache, in a good way. Before I even register what's happening, I blink, causing a tear to roll down my face. When Nash notices, he's instantly at my side, wiping the tear away with the pad of his thumb.

"You are perfect, Tatum Moore."

Nash's lips graze over mine in what is probably the sweetest, most gentle kiss of my life. His hand slides around to the nape of my neck and I melt into his touch. Leaning back, Nash's body falls on top of mine. One arm props himself up while the other holds onto me. His hard chest resting on top of me is the comfort I didn't know I needed. I feel safe and cared for. His words echo in my head as his tongue makes its way into my mouth.

You are perfect, Tatum Moore.

This might sound pathetic and sad, but no one has ever said anything like that to me. It makes me feel … weird. Like what Nash and I are doing is slowly changing. Evolving into something I don't know how to deal with.

His lips move to my neck, nipping and sucking a path to my collar bone.

"You should stay," he mumbles.

It's so quiet that I choose to ignore it and pull his mouth back to mine.

"Tatum," he pants between kisses, "you should stay the night."

Okay, now I can't pretend I didn't hear that. Nash pulls back, staring down at me with flushed cheeks.

I shake my head. "I can't stay. You know that."

Nash's mouth turns into a hard line as he pushes himself off me. I stand to meet him, confusion covering my face. Nash struts over to the window, peering down at the winter wonderland below.

"It's been snowing like crazy. The roads are probably crap. I shouldn't drive in this."

"Okay." I grab my phone from beside our food. "I'll just call an Uber then."

Nash scrubs a hand down his face, letting out a frustrated sigh. "I meant we shouldn't drive in this. No Uber is going to be out tonight. Tatum, just stay the night."

"I can't," I huff.

"Why not?"

"Because of the rules. We made those rules to prevent situations like this."

His eyes narrow to tiny slits. "I think a blizzard voids the rule, don't you?"

I grab the brown bag the food was delivered in and begin to place selected containers in it. I don't have the energy to fight tonight. "No. The rules are there for a reason. I can't stay the night."

"What are you doing?" Nash gestures to the bag in my hand.

"Taking some food with me."

"So you'll take the free food, but not the free bed?" he says sarcastically.

I slam the bag down on the table. "I offered to pay for dinner, but you refused. Why are you being a jerk?"

"Because the weather is complete shit. Just stop being so damn stubborn," he yells.

Thoroughly pissed off now, I abandon my food, shove my feet into my boots, grab my coat, and am in the elevator before he can say another word. How can he turn into such an asshole so quickly? I get that he was trying to be nice, but we made the rules for a reason. Thinking back now, I can't remember the reason. Maybe it was so we didn't get too close to each other? I feel like that ship sailed earlier tonight when I ripped open my chest and showed Nash all its contents.

I stomp out of the elevator, pulling my jacket tight over my chest and storming out of the building. My feet stop moving and my head hangs when I can't even see the road. White covers every single inch of the world and instead of smiling at the sight before me, I growl in annoyance. Not only am I ticked off at the sight of snow, I now have to admit Nash was right.

Spinning around, I make eye contact with Jeeves. "Can you buzz me up?"

All my energy from a moment ago seems to vanish and Jeeves simply nods his head as he holds the door for me.

The elevator doors open to the penthouse and my eyes scan the empty room. Even the food is gone from the coffee table. I wasn't gone that long. I loudly knock on the wall.

"You win," I shout and Nash reappears from his bedroom, sans shirt and pants. He's standing before me in only tight black boxers that leave nothing to the imagination. I have to force my eyes up to his face and it's one of the toughest things I've ever done.

"I win what?" he asks in a husky voice.

"I'm staying," I bark. Still angry, I let my coat fall to the floor and slip off my boots in the middle of the pristine floor. I walk by Nash, carefully avoiding touching any part of his body. I hear him sigh, probably at my snow-covered attire on the floor, but I ignore him. My steps halt when I see he has already laid out an oversized T-shirt and pajama pants for me.

"You can change in the bathroom," Nash says as he walks around me to get into his room. He's pulling a blanket and his pillow off the bed.

"What are you doing?"

He exhales sharply. "I'm sleeping on the couch. This way we're not breaking your oh-so-precious rule."

My head jerks back at his tone. Why is he so pissed at me? I came back, didn't I? Unless ... Does he want me to stay? Like, not just because the roads are crap, but for a different reason? Originally this was supposed to be just sex, but what if it isn't anymore? What if something more is going on here and I've just been ignoring it?

My hand flies up and lands on his chest when he tries to walk by me again. I look up to find him staring into the living room. Using my forefinger and thumb, I grab his chin and guide him so our eyes meet.

"Stay with me." It's almost a whisper, but I know he hears me. I watch as every defense he has put up in the last few minutes crumbles to pieces.

Nash's hands go to my waist, inching my shirt up. I lift my arms, allowing him to pull it over my head. He reaches for the shirt he laid out for me and helps me dress. I drown in his clothes and I love it. Pulling the shirt up to my nose, I inhale his scent, all man and Nash. He chuckles before climbing into bed, hugging his side. We both stare straight ahead, not talking to each other. When Nash's foot travels to my side of the bed, I turn to meet his eyes.

"Hi," he whispers.

"Hi," I say back.

Nash and I fall asleep, his chest pressed against my back. The weirdest part about this whole situation is that it doesn't feel weird. It feels like home.

Waking up Saturday morning, Nash and I are a tangled mess of limbs and sheets. I think I like it, opening my eyes and having his arm splayed across my belly like he enjoys having me here. There's the briefest moment when we're both still half asleep, just looking at one another. It feels comfortable. As if I could wake up next to him again and again.

Brendon is super sweet, but I don't think I could feel that way about him.

Stripping my clothes off after sneaking out of bed, I drop each article on the floor before pulling my hair into a bun. Carefully walking around the glass doors of Nash's walk-in shower, I turn the faucet to the hottest setting. After testing the water with my hand, I wait until the temperature is perfect, then step under the waterfall stream. When I turn to look for his soap, I slip on the slick stone, catching myself moments before I'm almost thrown through the glass walls. My heart races at the thought of having to explain that to Nash. Shelves holding various bath products line the sleek marble walls and I think I may never leave this room.

Grabbing the soap bottle off the shelf, I bring it to my nose and inhale. It smells like the ocean and Nash. My eyes open when I hear footsteps behind me.

Hands skim up my ribs, cupping my breasts, and Nash whispers, "Are you smelling my soap?"

I giggle, relaxing into his body. "So what if I was?"

I whimper when his hands leave my body, taking the soap from me. I start to spin towards him when one hand spreads out over my belly, holding my back to him.

His tone is low and husky. "Lean forward and hold onto the wall."

I do as he says, my fingers spread on the cold marble. I look over my shoulder and see his eyes staying on me as he squirts the soap into his hand. His fingers rub the soap into my skin, massaging my muscles as he moves lower. And lower. I squirm under his touch and gasp when he falls to his knees.

"Nash—"

"How did you sleep?" he asks, rubbing my ass.

"What? You're asking me this now?"

His tongue darts out to lick a part of me that has never been licked and my legs shake, almost giving out. "I asked, how did you sleep?"

"Good," I pant. "Good."

I feel his smile on my skin. "Me too."

The muscles in my arms struggle to hold me up when he licks me again while one hand snakes around my front, sliding one finger inside me.

"Oh, my God." I gasp for air when he adds another.

"Spread your legs for me," he breathes. It takes my brain a few seconds to process his words and when I do, he pulls my hips closer to his mouth. He kisses me gently, applying the smallest amount of pressure as his fingers pump in and out of me. Every stroke of his tongue sends a jolt of electricity through my body. My heart is pounding in my ears and every single muscle in my body spasms as I explode.

Nash kisses his way up my spine, leaning over me. "You have the most beautiful body."

Helping me stand up, I spin around and wrap my arms around his neck. "That was, I mean, I've never …"

He silently chuckles. "What I'm hearing is that you're happy you stayed the night."

Eighteen

Ignoring Mila's pleas, I stayed in last night. Trey's friend is in some band that was playing downtown and Mila spent at least thirty minutes badgering me before giving up. I spent the night cuddling with a glass of white wine under the weighted blanket in bed while I watched trashy reality television. It was amazing. I didn't think about work. I didn't think about drama with my family. I definitely didn't spend the night thinking about Nash's hard bare chest pressed against mine. Okay, maybe that last one is a lie. I did, however, think about dating Brendon while sleeping with Nash. And how it doesn't seem fair to either guy.

When I woke Saturday morning, Nash and I were both tangled in each other. There was the briefest moment when we were both still half asleep but just looking at one another. It felt comfortable. As if I could wake up next to him again and again. Brendon is super sweet, but I don't think I could feel that way about him.

I press my fingers to my temple when my phone rings. Why can't she get the hint? I roll my eyes, knowing the calls will only continue. Maybe if I answer and she says her piece, she'll finally stop.

When my phone rings for the third time this morning, I take a deep breath and swipe my finger across the illuminated screen.

"What?" I snap, not feeling at all bad for my harsh tone.

"Tat-Tatum? Sweetie, is that really you?" My mother, I mean Susan, sounds breathy, as if she's trying to make herself cry.

"Who else would be answering my phone?"

"Oh, honey. I just—I mean, it's just been so long. How are you?"

I can just picture her now. Sitting in some RV, probably at the Grand Canyon or some other touristy place, clutching her chest as if this is some memorable moment we're about to share.

"How am I?" Sitting up straight in bed, I run my free hand through my hair. "You really want to know how I am?"

"Of course. Tatum, I am your mother."

Something inside me snaps. Like, I can physically feel the crack beneath my ribs. "My mother? You haven't been my mother in a very long time and you know that! You know what? I'm great. Talk to you in another ten years."

My fingers are about to slam on the red button to hang up when I hear her yell, "Wait!" I turn the speaker on, setting the phone down on my comforter.

"I'm waiting," I say dryly.

Susan sighs deeply into the receiver, causing me to roll my eyes. "Tatum. Darling. I know we aren't there with you, but that doesn't mean we have forgotten about what month it is. Have you been to see Jules recently?"

"You don't have the right to say her name." My voice shakes with anger.

"Tatum Mallory Moore!" she scolds. "I thought we were past this. Jules's death was an awful event—"

"That you could have prevented!" I shout, waving my arms dramatically. "God! When was the last time you visited her grave?"

Her tone turns cold. "If you remember correctly, your father and I weren't even there. We were—"

"And that's the point! You weren't there! You were never there!" A hard lump forms in my throat, but I force it down. I will not cry. She doesn't deserve it.

The silence is deafening and I debate hanging up the phone again. This is the exact reason why I never answer her calls. All she wants is to have a normal conversation, but I can't do that. I can't move past the fact that my sister is dead.

"Tatum. I didn't call to fight," she says, her voice softening. "I called because I miss you. We miss you. It's been a long time. Too long. Your father and I are headed to Vegas next week. Why don't you come meet us? We can celebrate the new year in style. How does that sound?"

You know that little ball that forms in the pit of your stomach when anger begins to take over? Well, take that and make it about ten times bigger. Susan is going to regret calling me.

"You are un-fucking-believable! Jules's anniversary is right around the corner and you want me to celebrate by getting drunk with you two? How the hell did anyone ever let you be parents to one kid, let alone two? The nurses should've taken one look at you and wheeled my bassinet away. I don't understand why you keep calling! Why do you keep pushing? Don't you get that I have zero desire to be around either of you? Don't you understand that maybe, just maybe, if you were there that night, then Jules wouldn't have sneaked out?"

The words fell out of my mouth at lightning speed, and now I'm gasping for breath. Susan stays quiet. A wise move on her part.

"I was only eighteen years old," I continue. "Who makes good choices at that age? Let me ask you a question. Did you ever stop and think about how Jules and I grew up? It sure as shit wasn't because of your and Dad's superior parenting skills. I did it. Me. I was forced to be a mother to my baby sister because my parents weren't there. In eighteen years, I made one single mistake and it was the worst thing that could've happened. But the thing is, it wouldn't have happened if you and Dad were there. If you just stayed home and played the roles of our parents. I don't understand why it was so hard to love us."

Angry tears race down my face as my fingers twist and tug my hair. My shoulders start shaking and I cover my mouth, hiding my sobs. When neither of us speaks, I start counting.

One, two three ...

Eleven, twelve, thirteen ...

Twenty-one, twenty-two, twenty-three ...

When I reach thirty and not one word has been said, I press end. Falling back onto my pillow, I feel as if I'm drowning. The air around me has become too thick to swallow. How can she just pretend as if nothing happened? I still am not able to comprehend how a grown adult does not have any remorse about their daughter's death. My eyes flutter closed and I'm brought back to the horrible day.

It was mid-January. Before I went to bed, I texted and called Jules repeatedly. Jules always sneaked out with her boyfriend, Stan, but she'd never stayed out that late before. Sleep quickly took over me and I was awakened by a shrill ringing in my right ear. I can still hear the echo of my old ringtone every time I think about Jules. When I answered, it was a policeman. He said his name was Officer Manuel. I remember his face like it was only yesterday. His pinched furry black brows; sad, hooded emerald eyes; drawn-down corners of his mouth. I, a teenager, had to call our parents to tell them the news. The awful, horrible news. I can't remember if they were in Vermont or Maine, but it was one of the two. I have no memory of how, but the next thing I knew, I was at the police station. The constant noise surrounded me and I wanted to scream. Everyone was continuing on with their lives like my sister didn't just leave this Earth. I was crying so hard that I couldn't even stand up straight and I crumpled to the floor.

Two days later, we had Jules's funeral. It was like it was happening in slow motion. As if I was in a horrible nightmare and just needed to wake up. It took me around three months to realize I wasn't dreaming. That my baby sister was gone and never coming back.

Hurling myself out of bed, I run to Mila's room and throw open the door. When all I see are crumpled sheets tossed around the empty bed, my legs collapse. I slide down the wall, hugging my arms around me and desperately sucking breath in between sobs. Before I register what I'm doing, I brush my teeth, throw my hair into a messy bun, and get dressed in the black sweatshirt and sweatpants I stole from Nash. I'm about to leave the house when I see a sticky note on the wall beside the front door.

Went out for breakfast. Didn't want to wake you. Will bring you back bacon and eggs.

-XO Mila

Nineteen

My feet move quickly past Jeeves as I run towards the elevator. Once I step in and the doors shut, I see the button for the penthouse already glowing.

"Thanks, Jeeves," I whisper.

My leg shakes in anticipation as I continue to pick at my fingernails. I'm not even trying to not cry anymore; the tears are just automatically flowing down my cheeks. Pulling the sleeves of the sweatshirt over my hands, I frantically wipe away the water staining my face. As the doors open, a sigh of relief escapes my lips. Nash is standing in the doorway, holding a bowl of cereal with a puzzled expression. Brows pulled together, forehead creased, head tilted.

"Tate, are you okay?" He speaks softly.

I don't know how or why, but at those words, I fall to pieces. He tosses his bowl on the coffee table, a small amount of milk sloshing out and splattering on the glass. He wraps my arms around his waist and I bury my head into his chest as I soak his shirt with my uncontrollable sobs. The last time I cried this much was when Jules died. I was so hurt and betrayed that all I felt was numb. My entire body shivers and Nash pulls me tighter against him as he strokes my hair.

"Shh, shh. Sweetheart, you're okay. I got you," he purrs into my ear.

I'm not sure how long we stand there, but it has to be at least fifteen minutes. Nash scoops me up in his arms, walking me to his room and setting me down on his bed. He tucks me under the covers before climbing in on the other side. His hand cups my cheek as his thumb wipes away a rogue tear.

"How can I help?" he whispers.

Grabbing the hand on my face, I turn my head towards it and kiss his palm.

"Did I ever tell you why I'm so nutty about Christmas? Why I wear the ridiculous clothes and am so obsessed about something as stupid as the weather?" I mumble.

"It's not stupid."

A shy smile crosses my face for a second when Smelly Cat joins us in bed and instantly runs over to me, purring like crazy. "Jules loved the holidays, mainly Christmas. My parents weren't ever around, so we would do stuff together. Make gingerbread houses, go see light displays, stuff like that."

"Jules?"

I nod, slowly exhaling. "Jules is my sister. Well, she was my baby sister. She died ten years ago. Every December, it seemed like all the stuff she wanted to do was another chore to check off my list. I mean, our calendar was always jam-packed and I never had a second to breathe. When she died, I guess I started to see the magic she saw."

I watch as another tear lands on the white comforter. Twisting my fingers into the fabric, I pull the blankets around me. The words I want to say, the ones I've been suppressing for years, are begging to escape my lips. Focusing my gaze on the comforter, I open my mouth. I can't bear to look at anyone, let alone Nash, when I admit the truth.

"I blame my parents for Jules's death. I have for the past ten years, but it's not their fault. It's mine. I killed Jules. I was so young and stupid and I wasn't paying attention. She thought she was in love and it scared me. I was so nervous she would get pregnant and end up being like our parents. Always absent. Jules asked if she could go out with her boyfriend and I told her no because it was a school night. Looking back, I should've known something was up when she didn't press the issue. She just nodded and finished eating dinner. It was spaghetti and meatballs. I burnt the meatballs and they were truly awful."

I slowly inhale through my nose, exhaling through my mouth. "I had just gotten out of the shower when I heard the obnoxious roar of Stan's dad's sports car. Stan was her boyfriend. I ran out the door in my freaking towel to catch her, but they were already gone. I texted and called at least a hundred times, but never got a response.

Finally, I somehow fell asleep, only to be woken up by the police calling. They said Jules and Stan were in a head-on collision with a semi-truck. I was told they were both dead upon arrival."

Looking out of my peripheral vision, I see Nash's mouth slowly drop open. I close my eyes, waiting for the blow. Waiting for Nash to tell me how awful of a sister I am. How any normal human being would have been able to watch their little sister and keep them safe. Nash grabs my chin, turning my head to look at him.

"Nash. Don't."

"Please, look at me," he begs and I open my eyes.

"You have to know Jules sneaking out wasn't your fault."

I shake my head, feeling the too-familiar sting of tears.

"Tatum, sweetheart, listen to me. She was a child, but so were you. I need you to hear me. Jules's death was not your fault. It was an accident. Accidents happen."

"But it wouldn't have happened if I was paying closer attention! It wouldn't have happened if my parents had been there to stop her," I sob.

Nash slides closer to me and the bed dips under, accounting for his weight. He cups my face before our lips meet.

"It wasn't your fault," he murmurs. "I need you to know that you are not responsible for your sister's death."

I don't say anything, just continue to blankly stare at the freckle on his shoulder. Nash pushes a rogue strand of hair behind my ear.

"Where were your parents?" he cautiously asks.

I laugh, but there's no humor in it. "Where weren't they? When I was fifteen, they bought an RV and left. Their dream was to travel the world, just not with their children. They would sometimes call, but not often. I was only two years older than Jules, but I was forced to become a mom. I'm not sure how, but my parents continued to make money and would send us a couple hundred dollars every week. I just can't help but wonder—if they were there, would she still have sneaked out? Could they have stopped her?"

Nash leans back against his pillows, pulling me onto his chest. I breathe in his scent of vanilla and somehow feel calmer. His one hand rubs up and down my arm, the other grazing over the bare skin on my lower back. Hiccups continue to leave my mouth, but I think I am completely drained of all tears. I guess crying for hours on end will do that to you. Just as my breathing returns to semi-normal, I remember that Nash doesn't have a normal work schedule. He was having breakfast when I arrived and was shirtless. Was he eating quickly before jumping in the shower? I am the worst person ever!

"Oh, my God! Are you supposed to be at work? I completely forgot. I am so sorry! I just burst into your house and—"

Nash presses his lips to mine, effectively silencing me.

"I want to be here. Work is completely fine without me. Now, just relax and keep breathing."

Nash guides my head back to his chest, running his hand through my hair and massaging my scalp. The sensation is almost orgasmic. I then remember that even though we're now friends, I shouldn't be here. Anytime we've hung out before, it always ended in sex. We've never gone to each other for comfort before. Another reason I should've called instead of impulsively racing over here. I brace my hand on Nash's chest to push myself off him. He knows what I'm doing because he tightens his grip on me.

"Just relax, Tatum. I've got you."

My eyes squint open, taking in my surroundings. I must've fallen back asleep. I'm lying on my side, cuddling the blankets, and when I turn over, I frown. Where's Nash? My head pounds from dehydration and I take a deep breath before sitting up. I roll my neck from side to side a few times before massaging the sides with my fingers.

"How are you feeling?" Nash asks. He stands in the doorway, this time wearing a plain white T-shirt with his jeans. Damn, he's sexy. If my head wasn't splitting open and my face stained with dried tears, I'd try to seduce him.

"A little headache," I groan. He walks in further, producing a glass of ice water and three orange pills. I thank him before placing the tablets in my mouth and guzzling the entire glass. My eyes flutter shut, and I revel in the feel of cold water on my raw throat.

"What time is it?" I croak.

"Two in the afternoon. You needed the rest."

My fingers rub my temples as I make eye contact with Nash. "I am so incredibly sorry. I should have never come over without calling. I feel like I violated some unspoken rule. It will never happen again."

A deep V forms between his eyebrows and I shove the covers off myself.

"What do you think you're doing?"

"I need to go," I say, sliding off his expensive sheets. I try to walk to the door, but he barricades me between the wall and the bed.

"You are not going anywhere. I want you here. There's no unspoken rule. I'm honored that you chose to talk to me. I don't want you to leave. Now, will you please stay? I have an entire evening planned for us."

His words make my insides turn to goo and I hop back in bed. "What kind of plans?"

The smile that spreads across his face brings out his dimple. I love his dimple.

"There is a *Die Hard* marathon on. Now, I know it's a very controversial topic, if *Die Hard* is a Christmas movie, but—"

"It most absolutely is! I'm sorry, but if you don't watch Hans Gruber fall to his death off Nakatomi Tower at least once during your holiday, I feel bad for you."

Nash's lips part and I catch the tip of his tongue quickly dart out. "I think I'm in love."

We laugh as he climbs into bed and finds the correct channel. I rub a hand on my chest, wondering what this weird sensation is. My heart feels heavy, like a jolt of electricity was just sent through it. Obviously Nash is joking about being in love, but his words seem to make my insides feel all gooey. Cuddling with Nash while watching a Christmas classic feels ... right.

Watching the credits roll, I nibble on my lip. Part of me is in awe that I told Nash about Jules, but the other part is happy I did. I thought he was going to judge me and tell me what an awful person I am. Instead, he gave me comfort and reassurance.

"It wasn't your fault."

"I need you to know that you are not responsible for your sister's death."

I want to believe him. But if it isn't my fault, then whose is it? I know I've been holding a grudge against my parents, but maybe it truly is all their fault. I mean, if they were just present more, she obviously wouldn't have sneaked out. Right?

"I don't talk to my parents," I whisper.

"Huh?"

I push myself off Nash's chest. "I said I don't talk to my parents. I mean, I just did but that's not the norm. My mother calls all the time, but typically I ignore her calls. That's why I got so jumpy when you started asking me personal questions. I picked up their call today and that was how all this transpired." I gesture to my entire body.

Nash's hand finds my knee as I continue. "I know I resent them for being absent, but I think I blame them because I'm too scared to tell them the truth."

"And what's the truth?" His thumb moves back and forth.

"That if I were more responsible, Jules would still be here."

He releases my knee, sitting up straighter. "I need you to hear me when I say this. Okay?"

I nod.

"Jules was a teenager who wanted to hang out with her boyfriend. Regardless of if it was you or your parents, she still would have sneaked out. Jules wasn't like you. You were forced to grow up at an early age, but you made it possible for Jules to be a kid. And kids make mistakes. Her leaving that night was a mistake. I hope you don't hate me for saying this next thing, but I think it needs to be said."

My lips part in anticipation. What else can he possibly say?

"I don't think anyone is to blame for Jules's death. I think it is a tragic accident, and that's it. I'm sorry if you don't want to hear that. From what it sounds like, you should be mad at your parents for a lot of things, but not for this."

Wow. I did not expect that. I take a deep breath, trying to process everything Nash just said. I know I'm ten years older now and should probably have thought more about this, but maybe he's right. Maybe it wasn't my fault. I do suppose that if I was a normal teenager at sixteen and wanted to go on a date with my boyfriend, I might have sneaked out too. Reaching up, I stroke Nash's cheek before pressing my lips to his. His hands rest on my hips when I lean over, straddling him. I arch my back, trying to deepen the kiss, when he pulls back.

"What's wrong?"

Nash brushes his finger along my cheek before running it through my hair. "Can we just be together tonight? Like just cuddling and shit?"

I'm completely caught off guard at his words. I know he's rejecting my advances right now, but it doesn't feel bad. It feels like he wants to take care of me. I honestly don't know anyone, besides Mila, who has tried to take care of me.

I smile and laugh. "Cuddling and shit sounds great."

Twenty

Walking out of Nash's apartment this morning is harder than it usually is. Waking up, I feel emotionally drained and want nothing more than to just hide under the covers. Instead of pestering me to talk to him, Nash just slides closer to me and pulls me into his embrace. I only force myself up when my phone rings for the fourth time. Only one of the missed calls is from Susan; the other three are from my boss, Sienna Halls. After a quick phone call in which I lie and say I have the stomach flu—Sienna's a hypochondriac—I get ready to leave. Walking out the door may sound simple enough, but it's like last night changed something in Nash and me. A plethora of hugs and kisses are exchanged before I rush into the elevator.

"Tater Tot!" Mila shouts the second the front door shuts behind me. I sent her a text message last night explaining I wasn't coming home. When she asked why, I gave her a summary of my conversation with Susan.

Mila rushes me, wrapping me in the tightest hug I've ever gotten.

"Are you okay?" she mumbles into my shoulder. "What did that bitch do now? Just give me her location and you will be completely innocent if the police question you."

I laugh out loud at her absurd suggestion. She follows suit before tucking a loose strand of hair behind my ear. Wrapping her arm around my shoulder, Mila leads me to the couch.

"Do you want to talk about it?"

My phone dings with an alert.

> N: Just wanted to make sure you got home safely. My bed is pretty lonely without you ...

A shy smile forms before I remember Mila asked me a question. "Actually, no. I think I'm okay. Well, as okay as I can be. Last night I went to Nash's and we talked. It was ... amazing."

Her eyebrows raise. "Amazing, huh? I knew the doctor couldn't be all bad."

"He just listened and comforted me. We didn't even have sex. We just cuddled and it was nice."

Mila's eyes glisten and a smile takes over her face. "Tater Tot, that sounds amazing. You know what else that sounds like?"

I hold my finger up. "Don't say it."

"Love."

I roll my eyes. "It can't be love. We haven't known each other long enough to be in love. Plus, we're just friends."

"Oh, so now you're actually friends? I thought it was all just about sex."

Leaning into the cushion, I sigh heavily. "Why do you have to make everything so difficult?"

"Because I'm your best friend and your roommate and your maid of honor when you and Nash get married."

I bark out a laugh. "You are insane. I am not getting married to Nash. I don't feel that way about him at all."

"No?"

I shake my head.

"Answer me this," she continues. "When you weren't able to talk to me, who was the first person who came into your mind? Who was the person you were willing to trust with your most personal thoughts?"

I open my mouth but freeze when I register what she's getting at. My voice is barely a whisper. "Nash."

"And who have you been going on these elaborate holiday-themed dates with? The ones when you come home with the biggest smile on your face?"

"Nash," I groan.

"And who are you in love with?" Her expression softens at her last question.

There is no way I am in love with Nash. We've only known each other for a few weeks and could barely stand each other early on. Plus, I'm still seeing Brendon. I'm having fun! Wasn't that the entire point of the dating apps? I can't be in love with Nash. It's not possible.

My eyes travel up to Mila's. I swear she has superpowers because the second we lock gazes, my mouth opens again. "Nash."

My hands fly to my mouth in shock. "I'm in love with Nash?"

"You're in love with Nash."

She says these words so matter-of-factly. Like it's a completely normal thing for me to be in love with a guy I loathed when we first met.

"Holy shit," I mouth. "What—what am I supposed to do?"

Mila leans in, smiling so widely that it reaches her eyes. "Go get your man."

My Uber ride is almost painful. The mixture of excitement and nervousness has my body shaking in anticipation. What if he doesn't say it back? What if he really only wanted this to be just sex? What if he tells me he loves me? I try to focus on that last possibility. When I pull up to his apartment building, I'm so eager to get out that I forget I'm buckled in. A choking noise erupts from my throat when I unbuckle the seat belt and free myself. Jeeves is waiting by the door with a curious look on his face, probably wondering why I left this morning only to turn around and come back a few hours later. I tip an imaginary hat to Jeeves and walk into the lobby.

My smile widens when my eyes land on Nash. His hair is still messy from this morning and he looks adorable. Did he have some weird intuition that I was coming back to see him? My heels click against the floor as I make my way toward my guy. My guy. God, that feels so good to say.

My steps falter when I see he's busy talking to someone. A tall brunette with thick curls down her back. She turns to look at something and I get a glimpse of her profile. Perfectly sculpted nose with a jaw that could cut glass. My mouth drops open and I think I feel my heart plummet into my stomach. The night Nash and I ate Chinese takeout and talked about our exes, he briefly described his traitorous ex-girlfriend. After I showed him a picture of Johnny, he showed me one of him and Sassy at some beach resort.

Nash smiles warmly while Sassy runs a hand through her hair. My eyes instantly go to the gigantic diamond ring on her left hand. I suppose she could be married to some poor man and I am overreacting right now. However, the ring looks strangely similar to the one Nash said he bought and never got back. Nash's pearly whites are on display as he guides her into the elevator, swipes his key card, and they both disappear.

What. Just. Happened? My legs feel like Jell-O and I reach for the first thing that can steady me. It's a brown and gold lamp that isn't very stable itself. The lamp crashes to the floor, causing a loud THUNK to echo throughout the lobby. My eyes widen and my hands fly to my mouth. I don't have to look around the lobby to know that all eyes are on me. Jeeves is suddenly at my side, his hand grazing my elbow.

"It's all right. Believe it or not, that happens all the time. Are you all right, Miss Tatum?"

I spin around and wonder if he saw what I saw. I apologize before running out of the building, careful not to break anything else.

I was the one who said we weren't exclusive. I was the one who said we were just having sex. But did Nash not feel what I felt last night? Mila is right. I'm an idiot. I think I've been in love with Nash for a while now.

Twenty One

Mila meets me in record time, rushing out of the car and pulling me to her.

"What do you mean, he was with another woman?" she shouts once we get into her car. "I think it was his ex. I guess I would've thought he would tell me if he was seeing someone else. Especially if it was her. How could he do this to me?"

Mila sighs before switching lanes. "Don't hate me, but are you asking how he could see someone else while sleeping with you and not tell you about it? Kind of like what you're doing with Brendon?"

My mouth drops open in shock. "That is completely different! First off, Brendon isn't my horrible ex. Secondly, Brendon and I aren't sleeping together—"

"Wait, did you catch them in bed together?"

"Well, no." I stumble over my words. "I just saw them going into the elevator together, but they looked plenty cozy."

She continues to stare at me.

"Why are you looking at me like that? It's not the same! Brendon and I haven't even kissed."

"I'm sorry, what?" Mila shrieks.

I shrug. "He wants to take it slow. He was married and now is struggling to get back into the dating pool."

"Yeah, I know that part. But you didn't tell me you haven't even kissed the man. Is that because of Nash?"

"Not everything has to do with Nash," I snap.

After a few moments of silence, I apologize. "Em, I'm sorry. I'm just in such a horrible mood. You're right. You're always right. Why do I keep falling for stupid men? First I wasn't good enough for Johnny, now I'm runner-up for Nash? What is wrong with me?"

Mila slams on her brakes causing my neck to jerk forward and the seat belt to dig into my collarbone.

"What the hell?" I shout, noticing that we're at a red light.

"I swear to God, I will beat you with my shoe if you ever say that again. There is absolutely nothing wrong with you. You are beautiful and the most amazing person I have ever met. Any guy would be lucky to be with you and if Johnny or Nash or whatever stupid guy is next can't see that, then they must be blind. You have no idea,

Tatum! You have such a pure heart and soul that you should not be the one questioning yourself."

Tears are now racing down my cheeks. Mila has always been my biggest advocate but she's never said anything as sweet as that.

"I love you, Em!"

"I love you too, Tater Tot!"

We lean across the console for an incredibly awkward hug when the driver behind us lays on their horn. Mila flips them the bird and hugs me tighter.

B: When can I see you next, beautiful?

I stare at the unanswered text on my phone until the backlight fades away. It's been two days since I showed up at Nash's apartment unannounced. It's also been two days since I've spoken to him in any capacity. Multiple texts from Nash have come through asking if I'm okay, but they all remain on "Read." He even sent me a picture of him and Smelly Cat cuddling in bed, telling me Smelly Cat misses me.

We said from the beginning that we were only having sex, nothing else. Logically, I have no reason to be hurt. However, my brain isn't choosing to listen to reason; it's choosing to listen to my heart. My heart is crushed and broken and bruised.

I've been in a funk the last two days and Mila, being a complete sweetheart, has tried to bring me out of it. The number-one Christmas activity she hates with every fiber of her being is decorating gingerbread cookie houses. She always says they are too complicated and messy and never turn out how they are supposed to. After my workday ends, I walk upstairs to find the kitchen table covered in wax paper with one gingerbread house kit sitting in the middle. I almost start crying again, but instead give her a big hug and started to get to work.

I wish I could say it was fun, but it's not. I mean, Mila and I entertain each other and it's a memory I will cherish forever; however, the actual gingerbread house never had a chance. We run out of icing mid-build, candy spills over every tile in our kitchen, and to top it all off, the cookies crumble in our hands. Still, I thank her for her efforts and we take a picture with our sad excuse for a house. Looks like our gingerbread men and women will be homeless this year. Whoops!

Re-opening my phone, my fingers type a message.

T: How's Friday night sound? I heard about a few restaurants putting small igloos outside for outdoor dining.

B: That sounds incredible! I'll pick you up at 7.

The workweek speeds by and before I know it, it's Friday. I have now not spoken to Nash in four days. I know that doesn't seem like a lot, but ever since we met, we've spoken almost every day. It just feels like a little piece of me is missing. Somehow Nash has wormed his way into every part of my life. For example, I tried to pick out adorable jingle bell earrings for tonight and it only reminded me of how Nash was always genuinely kind about my Christmas obsession.

After Brendon picks me up, we drive downtown to a new Thai restaurant. Keeping the theme of the holiday, half of the sidewalk in front of the building is taken over by little igloos, each big enough for four people. Brendon, being the gentleman, called ahead and made our reservations. There's a heater in the corner of the igloo, so I shimmy out of my jacket before placing my napkin on my lap. It's such a cozy and intimate spot and it kills me when my mind imagines Nash sitting across from me instead of Brendon. I shake the thought out of my head. It's not fair to think about another man while I'm here. Nash probably isn't even thinking about me. He's probably busy with Sassy and that giant rock weighing down her left side.

Brendon and I order a bottle of white wine and clink our glasses together when it's delivered. I'm in the process of perusing the menu when Brendon clears his throat, causing me to look up.

"I was wondering if we could talk for a moment," he starts, tight-lipped and with knitted brows.

"Of course. Is everything okay?" I set my menu down. Brendon reaches across the table, taking my hand in his. My eyes drift down to his touch and it doesn't feel right. It feels off. Not like it feels when I touch Nash.

"You remember how I told you I'm in the process of getting divorced?"

I nod slowly.

"I was so excited for our date, I hardly slept this week." Brendon's face falls. "Brinley contacted me yesterday morning. She asked if we could get coffee." Pulling his hand away, Brendon rubs the back of his neck like he's not sure how to continue.

"Brendon?"

"We slept together last night and again this morning. I am so sorry. I know I wanted to take it slow and I told you Brinley and I were separated, which we were, but things have changed very quickly. We talked. Like, actually talked. We never did that when we were married. We have decided to get back together and I couldn't bear to tell you over the phone. I thought this needed to be done in person."

My eyes refuse to blink as my jaw hangs open. Out of all the scenarios I could imagine, this was not one of them. My breathing is slow and even as my brain tries to process everything he just told me. I'm definitely not mad since I've been sleeping with someone else too. Maybe I'm shocked and a little ... relieved?

"Wow. That was a lot of information." I grab my wine glass, taking a generous sip.

"Please don't be mad. I know that's such an absurd thing to ask. I just want you to know this isn't about you. Brinley and I have a very long and complicated history. I thought we had both moved on, but I was wrong.

A shadow moves past us on the sidewalk as Brendon grabs my hand and brings it to his lips. "I have enjoyed every moment we have spent together. There is some amazing man out there for you, Tatum."

One side of my mouth quirks up. "Thank you for being honest. I do hope you and Brinley have a wonderful life together."

Pushing my chair out, I stand. Brendon mimics my motion.

"Oh, please don't leave. Let me at least pay for your dinner. I owe you that much." His heart is so pure. There's no way I could be mad at him even if I wanted to.

"I appreciate it, but I should be going. Have a good night."

Sneaking out of the igloo, I wrap my jacket tightly around me as the wind picks up. I have been dumped a lot, but that was the nicest rejection I've ever experienced. Part of me wanted to hug him and ask if he was okay. As much as it sucks we didn't work out, I am grateful for getting to know Brendon. I'll miss him and his glasses.

I fumble for my phone, partially numb from the cold, and I dial Mila.

"Hey, babe! Date over already?" Her voice gets louder on the last word like she cupped her hand around her mouth and the receiver. The background is filled with holiday music and I realize why. I completely forgot Trey was taking her to Shopping in the Park, a tradition that downtown puts on every year the week before Christmas. All types of vendors flock to the park in hopes of selling the perfect present. A stage is set on the opposite side with local bands playing some cheerful music. Come to think of it, I'm only a few blocks away.

"Not exactly. Looks like Brendon's marriage isn't really over. He's getting back with his wife."

'What?" she shouts.

"I said, he's getting back together with his wife!" I yell into the phone. A woman walking by gives me a death stare and I move a little faster.

"Ouch. You okay with that?"

Closing my eyes, I take a deep breath, letting the cold air fill my lungs before I look up to the sky. A single flake falls on my nose.

"Actually, yes. As much as I'm pissed at Nash, I still love him. It's not fair to me, Brendon, or Nash for me to be playing with people's emotions when I'm not even sure of my own."

"That's very grown-up of you." The noise begins to fade and I wonder if she's walking away to hear me better.

"Are you guys going to be at the park much longer? I'm only a few blocks away and would love to see all the lights."

"Yes! Yes! Yes!" she shrieks. "There's a band with a super-hot guitarist and they are amazing!"

"Stop saying shit like that!" Trey hollers in the back. I hear Mila sigh and can picture her rolling her eyes.

"Be there in ten."

Shoving my hands deep into my pockets, I take my time walking through my very own winter wonderland. The snow has started to fall at a steady pace. The streets are empty and it's quiet all around. For someone who was just rejected, I can't help the grin covering my face. Strolling down the cracked sidewalk, my eyes focus on two teenagers holding hands. Few words are exchanged between them and they snuggle closer together. When we pass I make sure to tell them, "Happy Holidays."

My nose is completely frozen by the time I reach the park, but Mila's hug seems to warm me right up. We grab hot chocolate before exploring, Mila and I linking arms as Trey drags behind us. When he stops to look at a booth with tools of some kind, Mila pulls me along.

"You sure you're okay? I mean, I know how you felt about Brendon, but being dumped for the ex-wife or whatever still is rough."

I chuckle. "Yeah. It was a weird conversation and took me a minute to process it. Brendon was sweet, though. I almost thanked him for how pleasant the letdown was."

We both burst out laughing as my shoulder collides with a brick wall.

"Ouch!" I wince, looking up into the eyes I've been missing for the past few days.

"Nash," I whisper.

His clenched jaw and icy stare have me dumbfounded. Is he pissed? At me?

"Should've known you'd be here. I was just leaving," he huffs as he continues to walk away. I let go of Mila's arm and chase after him.

"Nash! Can we talk?" I shout at his back.

His hands pop the collar of his jacket, protecting his neck from the harsh wind. My walk turns into a slight jog and I somehow stub my toe on the hard ground. I fall forward, catching Nash's elbow with my hand. "Would you stop and talk to me?"

He spins in a flash. "You couldn't be bothered to pick up your damn phone this past week. What could you possibly have to say to me now?"

My mouth opens and only a squeak comes out. Even when we first met and didn't like each other, he never talked down to me like this.

"You know what? This is all fine. I don't want to get involved in this stupid drama."

He tries to walk away again, but I jump in front of him. "What drama? What is wrong with you?"

"Did you fuck him?" he shouts and I'm pretty sure a few people stop to watch. My head jerks back with confusion. Why would he ever ask a question like that? Oh no. I think I actually feel my heart crack. Who told him about Brendon?

"What are you even talking about?"

"That guy from the stupid igloo. Did. You. Fuck. Him?" He enunciates every word, taking a step closer.

"Nash, Brendon has nothing—"

"Oh, so he has a name? This mysterious man whom I've never heard of not only is holding your hand and kissing you in public but also has a name. That's just great." Every word is dripping with sarcasm and it's starting to piss me off.

"First off, we weren't kissing. Second, I don't think you want to go there with me."

"And why is that, sweetheart?"

I hate that he does that. "Sweetheart" is a nickname he calls me in the bedroom or when he's teasing me, not a word he can use to hurt me. That's not fair.

"Tell me about Sassy. Did you fuck her?" Hand on my hips, I steady myself. If he wants to play this game, so can I.

He squints and shakes his head. "What are you talking about? Wait. Were you, like, staking out my building or something? I thought you went home."

My jaw hits the floor. "So, it's okay to have sex with me and then have sex with your ex in the same bed as long as I don't find out about it? You are unbelievable!" I shout.

Nash turns to walk away before stomping back my way. "You—you think we slept together? You honestly think I would do something like that to you?"

He sounds wounded, but I'm too worked up. "Well, you looked pretty cozy entering the elevator together. I guess those feelings never went away, did they?"

Nash shakes his head as the vein in his neck pulses faster than I've ever seen before. "This coming from someone who has been screwing another guy behind my back. Kettle, meet pot." The calm in his voice is terrifying and sends a shiver running down my spine.

"I never even kissed Brendon!" I snap. "We went on a few dates and I wanted to tell you. I came to your apartment and then ... You know what? I'm not going to stand here and justify myself. We said we weren't exclusive. We made those rules for a reason."

"The rules?" His laugh is a mixture of anger and frustration. "The rules are crap and you know it! You should've just sucked it up and told me the truth. I thought something was happening between us the other night, but I guess it only makes sense. You not being able to follow through on something else in your life."

My eyes almost bulge out of my head. "Excuse me? What the hell is that supposed to mean?" I follow through on things all the time. Like ... well, nothing comes to mind right now, but I do.

"Seriously? You never follow through with anything! You tiptoe around your entire life and it's ridiculous!"

I take a step back from him. I think it would hurt less if Nash had punched me in the face. How dare he think he knows me!

"That's such a lie. You don't know a thing about me," I say through gritted teeth.

"Because you don't tell me anything! You were the one who wanted a rule that I couldn't ask you blatant questions! This is the theme of your entire life. Tell me, why haven't you published your book yet? Have you talked to your parents since the other night? Even if you had the slight thought that I was sleeping with Sassy, why didn't you just confront me like an adult?"

"Careful, Nash," I warn.

"It's because you're scared. Like a little girl and not someone who is almost thirty years old."

A pit forms in my stomach and I feel as if I'm about to faint. We've fought but never like this. His words have never been so sharp and hurtful. I want to cry. I want to tell him to stop and that he's hurting me. Instinctively, I wrap my arms around my midsection to protect myself from his next blow.

"I'm not scared," I manage to say, but my voice shakes. "You don't understand—"

"Then help me understand! That's all I've ever asked of you. I want you to tell me things. I want to be able to help, but you won't let me."

I shake my head when I feel the tears welling up in my eyes.

Nash takes a step closer and my voice comes out as a whisper. "We made the rules for this exact reason."

He scoffs. "Screw the rules and screw you, Tatum."

I look up in time just to see him vanish into darkness.

Twenty Two

My feet are frozen to the ground. Maybe I'm still standing here because I'm hoping Nash comes back? Or maybe it's because I don't know what to do next? That pit in my stomach turns into a black hole and I fear everything he said might be true. Tears cover my face. I'm quick to wipe them away, but they are just replaced with new ones. My chest feels hollow. My hand covers my mouth to hide my sobs when I feel arms wrap around my waist. Mila guides my head to rest on her shoulder as she tightens her embrace. Trey's strong hand lands on my shoulder and it only makes me cry more.

The temperature drops so ridiculously low that my tears feel like they actually freeze on my face. The two most amazing people in my life walk me to Mila's car. I try to protest when Mila slides in the back with me, but she ignores my words. When Trey puts the car in drive, the tears magically stop. I'm not sure if I've just cried out every inch of water my body has or something else, but my sadness has now been replaced with an emotion I am way too familiar with.

I feel numb.

Even though it hasn't been the most conventional relationship I've ever had, Nash has been everything to me lately. Yes, Mila is, and will always be, my go-to, but Nash had me thinking he could be my real soulmate. I have never talked about such personal things with another man, not even Johnny. Ever since Jules passed, I struggled to think about the future. Jules never got to plan hers, so why should I? Nash had me wanting to make plans.

My eyes flutter shut as I place my head on Mila's shoulder. I must've fallen asleep because the next thing I know, we're sitting in our driveway. Sitting up slowly, I roll my neck back and forth, resulting in a large crack. How long was I like that? Next to me, Mila's head tossed back and her eyes closed. The car is still on, but Trey is nowhere in sight.

Gently shaking her arm, I whisper. "Em. Get up."

She inhales through her nose and opens her eyes. Her hand stifles her yawn before she looks in my direction.

"Are you okay?" she whispers.

I shrug. "Where's Trey?"

Mila scratches her forehead before running her hand through her messy waves. "We got home and you were still out. I didn't want to wake you, so I told him to head inside."

She leans forward to see the clock on the dashboard. "That was about three hours ago. If you need my car tomorrow, you'll probably have to fill up the tank."

I shed more tears now as I leap across the seat and cuddle into Mila. "You are seriously the bestest friend in the entire world. I do not deserve you. I love you so much, Em!"

"And I love you, Tater Tot!" When I pull back and wipe my face, she asks, "Do you want to talk about it?"

"I know we weren't quiet. I guess you heard the whole fight?"

She nods with a sad smile. "Me and half of Pittsburgh."

A laugh bubbles out of my chest. "Not tonight. I think I just want to go to sleep. In my bed. Not that your car isn't comfy, but ..."

I let my sentence trail off as she climbs in front, turns the car off, and heads inside with me. Mila tucks me in before kissing my forehead goodnight. Sleep takes over my body moments later.

❄ ❄ ❄ ❄ ❄

Waking up Saturday morning with a hangover when I only had one sip of wine the night before is a cruel joke. My head feels foggy and when I try to swallow, I swear there's cotton in my mouth. I try to sit up, but a giant weight is holding me down and I don't have the energy to fight it. Sprawled in my bed, my mind replays last night's interaction with Nash. That was not at all how I wanted to talk to him about Sassy. Or Brendon. How did I let everything get so messed up? I should've just been honest with Nash about Brendon and told him about my feelings. I shouldn't have let Sassy mess things up between us. He sounded genuinely confused when I asked if he slept with her. But if they didn't sleep together, why would Nash's ex-fiancé be visiting him at his house? And why would they be holding hands in the lobby while she wears her engagement ring? It just doesn't make sense. I guarantee that anyone else who saw them assumed they were going upstairs to have sex too.

A light knock on my door pushes it open and I find Mila with a questioning look. I nod and she runs over, cuddling underneath the covers with me.

"The snoring stopped, so I figured you were awake," she mumbles. I grab the pillow behind my head and hit her with it, both of us laughing in the process.

"Seriously, though, did you get any sleep?"

"A little. I think."

Our hands find each other and the comfort is overwhelming. I have no idea how someone like me found someone as amazing as Mila for my best friend. She has always been there, no matter what, and I truly don't know what I would do without her.

"Do you think Nash was right? Am I scared to live my life?"

Her heavy sigh tells me her answer. I sit up, looking down at her with a horrified expression. "Oh, my God. You think Nash was right. I'm not a scared person, Mila."

"Just listen." She pushes herself to sit up before running her hands through her hair and gathering it into a messy ponytail. "I love you to death and I will always be honest with you. The reason I haven't said anything is because I don't want to push you. Everyone does things in their own time and you—"

"Mila!"

"Nash is right." The silence is deafening. "But I think it's just you taking your time, not that you're necessarily scared."

"Give me an example." I need to understand exactly what they are talking about. I am so unbelievably confused right now, it's not even funny.

"Do you want me to be sweet Mila or harsh Mila? I need to know what you're looking for."

"Definitely harsh."

Her eyebrows raise and suddenly I'm nervous about her next words.

"All right." Mila sits up straighter, staring me head on. "You finished your book three months ago. I know you did so don't try to deny it. I know you're a perfectionist and want the perfect ending, but you are always going to find problems with your words. You and I both know it's time to either self-publish or move on. Maybe start a new project. About Brendon—you should've told Nash. You've told me about your rules, but if you're being honest with yourself, you know those rules were more for fun than anything else. I do think you should've confronted him about Sassy instead of ignoring him, but

I understand why you didn't. And finally, I think you should talk to your parents."

My mouth drops open in shock. Of everyone in this world, I never thought Mila would ever utter those words.

She takes a deep breath. "You know I am in your corner and I always will be. Your parents messed up. They were absent and didn't take care of you. That is an acceptable reason to be pissed at them. You and I both know it was not your fault or theirs that Jules's died. It was a truly awful accident that was no one's fault. You said yourself that the roads were a mess that night and the truck slid into them. I completely understand how much easier it is to blame someone, but there's no one at fault. It was all just a horrible night."

Mila's uses her thumb to wipe across my cheek. I had no idea I was crying again until she pulls back her wet thumb, wiping it on her pajama bottoms.

"I don't want to hurt you. I never would want that. But you asked for harsh and so there it is. Do you totally hate me now?"

I shake my head. "Mila. I had no idea you felt this way. I could never hate you for being honest."

It's Mila's turn to cry as we embrace each other. This lasts until we hear the floor squeak under Trey's big feet as he walks into the room.

"I thought a threesome was off the table, but I'll take it as my Christmas present."

Mila pulls away, throwing a pillow and hitting him square in the face. We laugh as we wipe our faces dry.

Mila lets me borrow her car for a little alone time later in the afternoon. My fingers twitch when I see my phone sitting on my nightstand, but I decide to leave it. Nash hasn't texted me all day and I have no idea what I would even say to him if he did. When I pull into St. Mary's, I'm the only car in the lot. I drive around until I'm at my sister's final resting place. Putting the car in park, I step out and squat next to her tombstone.

"Hey, baby sister," I whisper before clearing my throat. "I missed you. Did you miss me? That's a stupid question. Of course you did. I'm your awesome big sis." A sad laugh escapes me.

I close my eyes when a gust of wind picks up. I know this might sound crazy, but I think I can feel Jules's presence. She's wearing her favorite olive-green cardigan and has her bleached-blond hair pinned up in a tight bun. She always had her hair in a bun so she could show off her extravagant earrings. I can smell the coconut body wash she loved. When she smiles, there's a slight gap between her two front teeth. When she was little, stupid boys would make fun of her for it. I saved up and told her I would pay to have it fixed but she refused. She said it made her look unique and she liked that. I liked that too. I always envied her confidence.

My shoulders start to shake. "Why did you sneak out? Why did you leave me? I needed you. I need you."

One of the nights Mom and Dad ditched us for some fancy dinner, we were eating popcorn and watching TV when we promised each other we would always be there. We would always take care of each other and never leave.

"I miss you so much, baby sister. I'm just so damn stubborn and I've been blaming Mom and Dad. Am I wrong? Would you still have sneaked out if they were there?"

Another big gust of wind knocks me off my feet. My butt lands in a wet pile of leaves, but I don't move. I reach out and wipe the snow off her stone.

"I'll take that as a yes. I suppose you got your stubbornness from me." I chuckle. "Mom called and I had it out with her. It just seems like they moved on with their lives so fast. I don't want them to forget you. I can't forget you. I won't ever forget you. God, I'm such a mess. Jules, what should I do?"

When the wind starts swirling around me, I stand up and open my arms in the air. "Okay. I get it. I know I always ask for a sign, but you can cool it. I'm not sure if they have gigantic warmers in heaven, but I'm freezing down here."

My eyes become huge when the breeze stops. Okay, that's freaky.

I sit back down and tell Jules everything, starting from the beginning. The dating apps, Nash, Cole, the ER visit, the casual sex agreement, Smelly Cat, Brendon, Sassy, and the epic fight that all of downtown got to hear. I'm out of breath by the time I'm done and my entire body is frozen, but I'm not ready to leave. I thank Jules for listening—she was always a great listener—and then start to rehash old memories. I find myself genuinely smiling and laughing in the cemetery. I probably look like a crazy person to anyone driving by. The sensation of having Jules here is back. It feels as if she's sitting right next to me, hand on mine and head on my shoulder. I look to my right and whisper, "You're right. You're always right. I love you so much, Jules."

Twenty Three

I can't remember the last time I spent that much time with Jules. I know that makes me an awful person. I know she wasn't actually there with me, but I felt like her spirit was. Answering my questions and telling me when I was wrong. When she was alive, she always knew how to put me in my place. Who knew that was a skill she would take to her grave? Okay, that joke may have been a little dark, but Jules would've laughed her ass off at it.

Driving home, I rehash Nash's words. He said I was scared. If I'm being completely vulnerable with my feelings, I guess I kind of am. I'm scared of things changing. My life was never perfect, but it was all right until I lost Jules. Maybe that's why I don't follow through on things like my book? I have everything in place and I even thought of a good ending. I think I'm scared that if I put myself out there, things can change and that might not be a good thing.

For some reason, Trey and Mila pop into my mind. Recently Trey has been spending a lot of time at the house and I can't help but wonder why. Every time, he comes over with a bag bigger than the last. He has a key and has been talking with Mila about taking their relationship to the next step. I'm already an emotional mess so why not add some more drama to my life?

Trey and Mila are cuddling on the couch when I get home and I plop down next to them.

Turning towards them, "Trey, can I ask you something?"

"Always," he answers right away. I'm directing my question to Trey on purpose because I know he won't sugarcoat his answer. Pushing my hair behind my ears, I take a deep breath.

"Do you want me to move out so you can move in?"

Mila's eyes pop open and Trey nibbles on his lip. "That obvious, huh?"

"That's not true at all!" Mila interrupts, darting her eyes between us. "I love you so much—"

"But you're in an adult relationship and want to move forward. I guess it's kind of hard to do that with a roommate." I don't mean for my tone to sound so glum.

Mila's brows pull together as Trey mutes the TV.

"T, you know we love hanging out with you. We just talk about the future. We're not sure if it's in this place or somewhere else." His hand scrubs down his face before it goes back around Mila's shoulders.

"We don't want to hurt you, Tater Tot," Mila whispers, placing her hand on top of mine.

I nod and stand up, wobbling as I walk away.

"Where are you going?" Mila cries.

Forcing a smile on my face, I turn back around. "I have a lot of stuff to do. Top of the list is apartment hunting. Thank you for being honest with me."

I leave my bedroom door cracked as I sit in bed and open my laptop. Half of me thinks I shouldn't have said anything because then I wouldn't be basically homeless. The other part knows I did the right thing by bringing it up. It's going to be weird living without Mila. She's been my constant for as long as I can remember. A single tear drops on my laptop and I wipe it away.

My eyes travel to the ceiling. "Is this you, Jules? Are you trying to get me to stand on my own two feet? You could've done it in a way that didn't completely uproot my life."

My laughing ceases when my door moves on its own.

"I swear to God, if you haunt me I will haunt your ass right back," I tell my baby sister.

Searching for apartments is more mind-numbing than I thought it would be. All the places that look nice in the pictures have horrible reviews and all the places I can afford, let's just say I'd have to make sure I'm up to date on my tetanus shot. After another thirty minutes of looking with no results, I know what I have to do.

Opening a separate tab, I pull up my novel. My fingers hover over the keyboard before typing out the title: *Love at First Fight*. I spend the next few hours toying with my cover: The female character sits at a coffee table sipping from a blue mug with her legs crossed. Her eyes are fixed on the male sitting across the way from her. I had it made a while ago, I just need to add the title in big beautiful blue letters. I've been slowly getting ready for this moment over the past few months. All that's left to do is for me to pull the proverbial trigger and I think—I mean, I know—it's time.

Sunday morning, I wake up bright and early. Before I can even think, I grab my laptop and press the start button. I'm shaking in anticipation as my browser loads. I chew on my nails as I watch the rainbow wheel of death spin around and around. When the ding of new email sounds, I freeze. My lips part as I process what I am reading. I officially published my book last night. It probably wasn't the smartest way to do it; I should've created a fan base and gone from there, but I knew if I didn't do it last night, I never would. Somehow I have sold three copies in just over twelve hours. How the hell is that possible?

An unintelligible noise escapes my lips and I quickly cover my mouth so I don't wake Mila and Trey. Oh, my God! I sold copies of my book. MY BOOK! Does this mean I can call myself an author now?

"You okay?" Mila whispers through my door and I tell her to come in. Her brows pinch together as she takes in the scene. Me, still with bedhead, dancing like an idiot with the biggest smile.

"I think I did it."

"Did what?" she asks through a yawn, crawling onto the edge of my bed.

"I self-published my novel last night and sold three copies overnight. I think I'm an author."

Mila's mouth falls open as her smile grows and her eyes gloss over.

"Hell, yeah, you're an author! I knew you could do it!" She screams and tackles me to the mattress. We both start shrieking and giggling to ourselves when Trey stumbles into the room.

"Why are you two being so loud?" he groans.

When Mila tells him the news, Trey looks directly at me. "You'd better be prepared because I'm only ever going to do this one time. Okay?"

Confused, I nod.

Trey rolls his eyes, takes a deep breath, and jumps up and down while clapping and cheering for me. I jump up and wrap my arms around his neck with Mila laughing so hard, tears spill down her face.

This is huge! I can't believe I did it! I would love for my words to make their way out into the world, but if all I ever sell are these three copies, I will be more than proud of myself. I did it! Mila insists we celebrate, so after a lazy day of doing nothing, all three of us get dressed up to go eat at Sushi, Sushi. As we're walking back to Mila's car at the end of the night, I steal a moment to myself. Looking up at the night sky and the few stars it holds, I whisper, "Thanks, baby sister."

❄ ❄ ❄ ❄ ❄

I've been staring at my phone for the past ten minutes, my fingers hovering over the green phone icon. Today is Christmas Eve. I should be happy, right? I think conflicted is a better term for what I'm feeling. Besides Mila being one of the first people I wanted to tell about my book, there is someone else.

My Mom.

Well, Jules too, but I'm pretty sure she already knows.

I think my mom will be proud of me. I hope she'll be proud of me. That's what parents do, right? Feel proud of their kids for big accomplishments? I hate to admit it, but Nash and Mila are right. I know they are right. It's just hard to say it out loud. My finger pushes the icon before I can turn back.

"Tatum?" a high-pitched voice asks.

"Hey, Mom."

I hear her sigh and I know why. I think the last time I called her Mom without being rude was before Jules died. Ten years ago.

"Hi, sweetie. Is everything okay?"

Closing my eyes, I see her hand go to her neck as she wraps her fingers around the necklace she always wears. It's a gold heart with little diamonds on the arch. My dad bought it for her the first Christmas they spent together.

"Yeah." My voice is soft and calm, the opposite of what it usually is when I'm on the phone with her. "I saw Jules the other day. It was nice to talk to her again. I don't go as often as I should."

"You know that you don't have to. Just because that's her final resting place doesn't mean she isn't with you all the time. She's probably listening to us having this conversation right now. You could talk to her just as easily in your kitchen."

My head jerks back while I register what she said. Holy crap, she's right! I know I haven't gone to Jules's grave as much as I should, but I have talked to her. I have thought about her constantly. My eyes look toward the sky and a shy smile forms.

"I don't think I've ever thought about it like that."

Seconds go by with neither of us talking. It's different this time, though. There's no heaviness weighing on the conversation. It's comfortable and appropriate for the situation. I feel like this is how it's supposed to be.

"I miss you," I mutter before I can stop myself. I need to be honest with them and as mad as I am at them for being absent most of my life, I still miss my mom and dad.

"Oh," she hiccups, "we miss you, too. You have no idea how long we have wanted to tell you that. Can we see you?"

Before I can answer, my phone rings with an incoming FaceTime call. My thumb twitches before answering it. A smile bigger than I've ever seen covers my mother's face. Dark chestnut hair that frames her sharp cheekbones. Honey golden eyes that look almost fake when the light hits them at the right angle. A few more wrinkles than I remember, but that's to be expected. My dad's blue eyes are blurry with tears. I remember when I was younger, he told me he hated his teeth and that's why he always smiled with his lips closed. Not today. His tinted and slightly crooked teeth bring a genuine smile to my face. My parents' skin is much darker than I remember. The sun must be intense wherever they are now.

"Wow," my mom breathes. "You are breathtaking, Tatum."

A tear rolls down my cheek. "So are you. Where are you guys?"

"Just rolled into the Grand Canyon not long ago. You would love it, baby doll."

My insides turn warm at my dad's nickname for me.

"Are you okay? You sound raspy," I direct at my dad.

He clears his throat. "Just a little congestion from the dust. For some unholy reason, I let your mother drive. Mistakes were made."

Dad and I laugh while Mom makes evil eyes at him. I don't know when was the last time we all laughed together. That's so incredibly sad.

"I want to tell you guys something."

They both lean closer to the camera.

"I self-published a book. It's a romantic comedy and I only published it last night, but it sold. Only a few copies. It's not exactly going to be on *The New York Times* bestseller list, but—"

"Holy shit!" my dad rejoices. "That's incredible! My daughter is an author. You have to send us a copy with your signature. I would love to place it on the dashboard so everyone can see our daughter is kicking ass and taking names."

For once, my tears are because I am so unbelievably happy. I wasn't sure what they would think about my writing, but now I don't know why I didn't tell them sooner. We spend the next hour talking about their trips around the U.S. They always planned to travel to all fifty states and as of right now, they only have Montana and the Dakotas left. When I ask them what their plans are for after they meet their goal, they talk about coming to visit me. They say maybe we could all take a trip to Europe or somewhere exotic. Dad jokes that I would have to pay for everything because by then I will be making millions off my writing. The conversation turns heavy when I bring up the night Jules died.

"Mom. Dad. I'm so sorry. I should've watched her. I should've checked up on her. I should've been a better sister—"

"Honey, shh," my mom says. "It wasn't your fault. We shouldn't have put so much pressure on you."

"Jules was a teenager. We were once all teenagers who made impulsive decisions. That night was just"—my dad clears his throat like he's trying to fight back tears—"a horrible, horrible accident."

I grab a tissue and dab at my eyes. The tears won't stop. I'm feeling weird. Almost lighter, if that makes sense. We reminisce on how amazing of a person Jules was and they praise me for being the parent they never were.

"You guys really do look good," I say through a sob.

My dad blows a kiss at the screen and I pretend to catch it, placing it against my heart. We make plans for another video chat after Christmas. I'm surprised when I find it difficult to end the call.

Without a word, Mila slips into my room and wraps her arms around me. I cry into her shirt for what feels like the millionth time this month. I never thought I would say this, but I'm so glad I was able to talk to my parents on Christmas Eve.

Twenty Four

A tradition I have upheld since Jules was alive is watching *How The Grinch Stole Christmas* before bedtime on Christmas Eve. I told her Santa would only come if she was sleeping, and somehow she convinced me every year that the only way she could sleep is if we finished the movie. Every year, we would make popcorn, cuddle in my bed, and watch the movie. More often than not, I would doze off, but her elbow would always wake me. She never said it out loud before she passed away, but I know she knew I was Santa. She was way too smart to believe mom and dad could buy all those presents when they barely knew her.

When the movie ends, I kiss Mila on the cheek goodnight and high-five Trey. I lie in bed for a solid thirty minutes before I give up on sleep. My mind is racing and as much as I try to focus on going to sleep, it isn't happening. The past few days have been quite eventful. However, for all the things I fixed, there's still one gigantic elephant pouting in the corner of the room.

The minute I got off the phone with my parents and was being pulled into Mila's embrace, I only had one thought in my head. Where is Nash? I want to run to him and tell him everything. Tell him the conversation with my parents was the best one we've ever had. Tell him I'm actually looking forward to them coming to visit. Tell him he was right and I was wrong.

Walking to the kitchen, I open the fridge and stare at our lack of food. Some old cheese, two beers, half-empty gallon of milk, and leftovers I can't recall putting in there. We really need to go to the grocery store. I wonder if Nash is having a late-night snack. Or maybe even a drink. 'Tis the season to celebrate and all.

My eyes instinctively roll when Trey's snoring reverberates off the walls. I sneak into my room, shove my feet into my boots, and grab my jacket. Mila's not going anywhere at ten at night on Christmas Eve, so after a quick text to her that I'm borrowing her car, I head out the front door. Her car is frozen shut and I have to use some serious strength to pry the door open. Bursts of condensation leave my mouth as the engine roars to life.

Most businesses are closed, considering what day it is. I decide to park in a garage close to Market Square and the ice rink Nash took me to. Making sure to tug my gloves on, I get out of the car and start walking. The second I emerge from the parking garage, white flakes start to fall. A smile crosses my face as I make my way. Not going to lie, I'm pretty cold. Although that doesn't stop me from enjoying the magic of snow on Christmas Eve. All I've ever wanted was to have a white Christmas. Not a small dusting of snow, but actual snow, so roads are slushy and everything is covered in a beautiful white blanket. The glistening of the crystals makes it look like you're staring at a painting. With the way the chunks are getting bigger, I think I'm finally going to get my wish.

Considering it's almost midnight, all the booths for vendors are closed but the lights are still turned on. My eyes travel up and down the pink and white Christmas tree made only of lights. It's breathtaking. Behind me, yellows, oranges, blues, and greens engulf Santa's village. A dusting of snow covers the fake tree and presents. I walk closer to the makeshift village but freeze when I hear the tap of footsteps on cobblestone. Who else would be out right now? I didn't think through coming downtown alone at night and not telling anyone where I was going. This is the definition of a face-palm moment. My hand reaches into my pocket and grips my phone tightly. If anything, I can hit the person over the head and run away.

The steps are too close, getting louder by the second. Then they stop. I turn around, hauling my phone above my head and shouting like a maniac. If I scream loud enough, someone has to hear me. My arm freezes in mid-air when I'm face to face with my apparent attacker.

"Were you seriously just trying to bash my skull in with your phone? It has glitter on it, for crying out loud," Nash teases.

My lips part in shock as I lower my arm, placing my phone back in my pocket. "What the hell are you doing here?"

He gestures to the empty square. "Wanted to go for a walk."

"In Market Square?" He nods. "At midnight?" He nods. "Where I'm just conveniently walking?" He nods again.

My arms spread wide, silently asking for him to explain.

"I wanted to talk to you," he simply says.

"Okay. Well, that object I was just about to kill you with works both ways."

His chuckle is low and dangerous. It sounds the same as when we would play fight, right before—

"So I might have been a total creep. I stopped by your place and Mila didn't know where you went. Told me her car was gone, so I put two and two together. I don't know if you know this, but we doctors can be pretty smart when we want to be."

His joke is cute and it takes all of my focus not to smile at him. I can tell he sees my mouth twitch because one corner of his perks up.

"I bet she was pissed you woke her up. However, that still doesn't explain why you're scaring the hell out of me in Santa's Village."

He nervously rubs a hand over the back of his neck, shifting his weight from one foot to the other. "Don't be mad."

No sentence ever that has followed the words "Don't be mad" turns out to be a good one.

"I may have talked Mila into using the Find My Phone tracker."

I don't even think. I step forward and smack his shoulder. Not too hard though, because as weird as it is, I'm somewhat flattered.

"You stalker!"

"It was for a good cause," he says, holding his hands up in defeat. "I wanted to apologize. I know my timing is shitty, but I needed to see you."

My arms cross protectively over my body. "You needed to see me? Maybe I didn't want to see you. You know, I'm known for not finishing things so I could've just ditched your ass and been done with it."

A puff of smoke comes from his sharp exhale. "I really screwed up. I was pissed and I let my anger get the better of me. I should never have said—"

I hold my hand up to stop him. "You don't need to say anything. I should—"

"Yes. Yes, I do. Tatum." Nash steps closer, taking my hands in his. "I was such an ass. I was that person you met on the first date. I never told you, but the waitress came by after you left. She said the bartender messed up your drink and wanted to refund you." He laughs at this and I bite my lip to keep a straight face. "I know we weren't technically together, but I would never cheat on you. When Sassy came over, it was nothing. After Sassy and I talked, I asked her to come over so I could get my ring back. I guess that's why she was wearing it; so she wouldn't lose it. I promise you, she left without the ring and it is now sitting safely in my deposit box at the bank."

I finally manage to look up at him. His eyes are glossed over and I feel my heart crack. I've never seen Nash so emotional. So raw and honest that I just want to comfort him and tell him everything's okay. I don't because even though he's being honest, it still doesn't wipe away all the horrible words he said to me.

"I shouldn't have lost my shit like that. I just thought ..."

His sentence trails off and his gaze goes above my head.

I tug on his hand, getting his attention. "You thought what?"

"After that night you came over and were upset, I thought things—I don't know. Changed? I know that probably sounds stupid now, but I think that's why I got so mad. I felt one way while you were still keeping your options open. It's my fault because you told me from day one that it was only sex. That's all I was good for—"

"Excuse me? I never said that's all you were good for. At first, you were just an outlet I needed. Don't you get why I made that rule in the first place?"

When he continues to stare at me, I blurt the words out before my mind stops me. "I made that rule because I didn't want to risk falling for you. A hot doctor who lives in a penthouse and has an adorable cat. What's not to love?"

"Love?" he breathes and I nod.

"I recently realized I have a lot of unresolved feelings about Jules and my parents. Jules was never able to make plans for the future. She didn't get that choice. She didn't get to be happy, so why should I?" He goes to say something, but I continue, "I should have told you about Brendon. Truly, what you saw was us saying goodbye to each other. I never even kissed him. We went on a total of three dates and

I'm such an awful person for saying this, but you were always in the back of my mind. I should've known then what I was feeling, but I've been told that I'm stubborn."

"Yeah, you are."

I purse my lips at his agreement and he gives me a reassuring smile.

"You were right," I practically whisper. "I don't finish things and maybe I am scared. The way you said it though ... You can't take back your words. It hurt me, Nash."

"I know, sweetheart." He cups my face with his hands. The cool leather gloves slide over my skin, sending a shiver throughout my entire body. "I will never lose my cool like that again. It was unacceptable. I was on edge from not talking to you and when I saw him holding your hand, well, I lost it. And that will never happen again."

"You're talking like there's a future for us," I mumble.

A deep V appears between his brows. "Who says there isn't?"

My eyes travel down to the ground when Nash releases my face. He takes a few steps back before shoving his hands through his hair, sending little specks of snow flying.

"Do you not understand how I feel about you? Sweetheart, I love that even though you're the most headstrong and stubborn woman I know, you're the most optimistic. I love how much you love Christmas and this season. I love your holiday spirit and how obsessed you are with freezing your ass off just so you can watch the snowfall. I loved going on those Christmas-themed not-dates dates. I love your

Christmas tree and candy cane and snowman earrings. But most importantly, I love you. And I think you love me too."

Nash approaches me, stopping only mere inches from my lips. "I will never stop apologizing for my behavior the other night. I promise to make it up to you in every way imaginable. I love you so much. Tatum, you are more than enough."

My heart melts inside and before I have time to think, I'm pulling Nash's face down to mine. His lips are ice cold, but I don't care. I press my body up against his as his hands wrap tightly around my lower waist.

"I missed you," he says into my mouth, his tongue moving in sync with mine. I don't know how I forgot about this. About how amazing it feels to be in his arms, pressed against him.

"Is there anything you want to say?" He pulls back, raising one eyebrow.

What is he talking about? I already apologized and—"Oh! Right! I love you, too!"

Twenty Five

My eyes flutter open and a smile crosses my face. It's Christmas Day. A gasp escapes my lips as the warm body behind me starts to move. Fingers drag up my ribs, moving around me to cup my bare breast.

"Merry Christmas, sweetheart," Nash whispers in my ear. His teeth nip into my skin as I arch my back to get closer to him.

After our picturesque make-up with the most perfect Christmas tree backdrop, and Nash assuring me Mila's car would be fine overnight, we stumbled our way to Nash's car. I'm pretty sure he ran through a few red lights as my hands traveled over his body. It's not my fault his muscles beg to be touched. We did run into the curb, but only once. According to Nash, I was being too distracting. Jeeves greeted us with the biggest smile before we raced into the elevator and up to his penthouse. After the door slammed shut, shirts, pants, and undergarments were tossed around the room. Our kisses turned hungry and needy. All teeth and lips and tongue. The filthiest words I've ever heard in my life were whispered against my skin. The night was spent under Nash, on top of Nash, in front of Nash. Let's just say my entire body is sore this morning and I'm not the least bit sorry.

"Merry Christmas," I moan as his fingers begin to work heavenly magic on my body. Looking back at him, my lips find his adorable smirk. His groan into our kiss is probably one of the sexiest sounds I've ever heard. Rolling over so our chests are pressed together, I reach down between us. A hiss escapes his lips when I wrap my hand around him. His head falls against the pillow and I bite my lip as I watch him come undone just by my touch.

"I love you," he murmurs before rolling me on top and quickly filling me. We move together as I place my hands on his chest. His hands continue to explore every curve my body has to offer. I feel Nash's legs tighten just as I find my release, not bothering to be quiet. Nash's penthouse takes up the entire floor. Who the hell is going to hear? Sitting up, Nash wraps his arms around me as we ride out each other's orgasm. Moisture coats his hairline, causing his messy hair to stick to his face. I smile as I push it back, running my fingers through it.

"You are amazing. You know that?" he asks between kisses to my nose, cheek, and jaw.

"I love you so much. However, you know that means there are now new rules."

He rolls his eyes and swats my behind. "What kind of rules?"

"Well," I say, guiding him back to a lying-down position. I cuddle under his arm, my leg thrown over his. "Number one. We are as exclusive as can be."

He continues my insane rules. "Number two, I get to ask whatever questions I want."

I giggle. "Three. Sleepovers every night, unless otherwise discussed."

Nash's body shifts under me and I look up at him. "Number four. You move in with me."

The playfulness that was in the air only moments ago turns serious. My lips part and I push myself to a sitting position. His eyes are intense and his perfect little dimple is out to play. He's not kidding.

My head swivels around the room. Could I see myself living with Nash? We've only known each other for a month, even though it feels like a year. What if he suddenly decides I'm too much and I end up homeless? What if ... wait, no! I'm not that person anymore. I don't need to question every decision I make. I deserve this. I deserve to be happy. If we were in our early twenties, I would think Nash was nuts. But we're not. We're old enough to know what we want and when we want it. I've never felt this way about anyone. Never felt this sure about any decision I've ever made.

"You're being serious?" I ask, hopeful that he is.

He slowly nods as his thumb grazes my jaw.

Wrapping my hands around the back of his neck, I pull his mouth to mine. "When can I start moving my stuff?"

Nash jumps on me, peppering my body with little kisses as his fingers assault my ribs. I can't stop smiling as I laugh so hard, tears spill from my eyes. When I finally wiggle away from Nash, I feel the sharp sting of his hand on my bottom.

I turn to glare at him as I get out of bed.

"Hey," he defends. "That ass is mine now. Get used to it." He lies back, propping an arm behind his head as he watches me disappear into the bathroom. Not sure how I didn't expect it, but once I reopen the door, Nash throws me over his shoulder and back into bed.

About two hours and another round of mind-blowing sex later, we finally manage to put some clothes on. Nash protests the entire time, but Mila is insistent with her calls.

"What the hell happened to you?" Mila demands after she picks up my call.

I huddle under a blanket in a chair in the corner of Nash's room, a huge smile still plastered on my face. "Shh, Nash is in the kitchen and you're so loud right now that you could probably wake the dead."

"Nash?" she questions and then starts cheering. "It's a Christmas miracle!"

"You are absurd," I laugh with her.

"So, tell me everything. About the make-up and the abundance of sex that followed it."

I bite my lip to keep myself from telling her every little detail. "Maybe later. I just wanted to call and say Merry Christmas to my best friend and her boyfriend."

"Merry Christmas, Tater Tot! Look, Trey said he's getting takeout from some fancy restaurant tonight for dinner. Just might know it. It's the Chinese place down the street." She laughs at her own joke. "You guys should stop over afterward. With booze!"

My shoulders shake from laughter. "We would love to!"

Mila tells me what time to come and I hang up. I see the MeetCute app and delete it without hesitation. I definitely won't be needing it again.

"Nash?" I call when I head into the other room and don't see him in the open space of his apartment. A small red box with a green bow sits on the end table and I walk towards it. Looking around and still seeing no sign of him, curiosity gets the best of me and I open the box.

"Oh, my." My mouth hangs open and my shoulders shake as I laugh. A pair of the most hideous and amazing earrings I have ever seen lie on crinkled white tissue paper. Trolls dressed as Santas with long furry green hair hang off golden clasps.

Hands wrap around my waist as Nash nuzzles the side of my neck. "Do you like them?"

"They are awful. I love them!" I continue laughing. "Where did you even find these?"

He nibbles my ear. "A vendor was selling these downtown and I instantly thought of you."

"I don't know if I'm flattered or offended."

Tossing the box down, I put the earrings on and spin around to find a very hot and shirtless Nash.

"I thought we said we were getting dressed," I say, crossing my arms so he doesn't get any funny or sexy ideas.

Ignoring my comment, he licks his lips. "I like the earrings."

Every single muscle is glistening under the lights and his jeans hang low on his hips. At first, his steps are slow, but when I catch on to his plan, we both start sprinting around the apartment. Me trying to get away from him and him trying to get me naked. It takes a whole five minutes for him to catch me and strip off all my clothing. He tosses me over his shoulder, and his hand colliding with my bare backside echoes throughout the living room.

"Where are you taking me?"

"To fulfill the dirtiest of my fantasies."

My eyes widen. "Which is?"

Nash lays me down on his kitchen table, pulling me to the edge. He runs his hands up and down my heated flesh and smiles when I quiver in anticipation.

Thrusting into me in one hard motion, he leans down and whispers, "Having my way with you on every single surface in this penthouse."

❄ ❄ ❄ ❄ ❄

With a lot of effort on my part, I finally get Nash fully clothed. As I'm herding him out of the apartment, an idea forms in my brain.

After we take the elevator down to the garage, Nash holds my car door open for me. I'm about to get in when I turn around and ask, "Are you okay if we make a quick stop before we head over?"

"Sure, where do you want to go?"

I give him directions once he settles in the driver's seat.

Twenty Six

No words are said as I point to where he should park his car. I can't tell how he's feeling right now and it's only making me more nervous. I reach for the door handle, but pause and turn to meet his gaze.

"This is too fast, isn't it? I'm sorry. I totally get it if you don't want to get out of the car. I just thought it would be—"

"Tatum," he interrupts.

I arch my brows in concern. "Yeah?"

"Take me to meet your sister."

Smiling sheepishly, I open the door and step into the cold. When Nash walks around to my side of the car, I stick my hand out for him to take. We walk slowly towards Jules, the grass crunching beneath our feet.

"Hey, baby sister," I mumble.

A single tear streaks down my face as Nash squeezes my hand tighter, assuring me he's here. "This is my boyfriend, Nash. He's the one I told you about."

Curious about how Nash is going to respond to the situation, I look up at him with knitted brows.

"I've heard only good things about you, Jules. I hope you can say the same."

A laugh bubbles in my throat and I know Jules is laughing too.

Nash clears his throat and squats, placing one hand on the ground. "You see, your sister here somehow convinced herself that we weren't meant to be. She kept insisting we were friends, blah, blah, blah. It took me until Christmas Eve to realize how important she is." Nash pauses and looks up at me. "That she is more than enough."

The sharp inhale of cold air burns my lungs and I mouth, "I love you."

"I love you, too." He turns his attention back to Jules's grave. "Sorry, that was meant for Tatum. But who knows, in another life—"

I smack his shoulder and he chuckles as he stands back up. Nash wraps his arm around my shoulder, pulling me closer.

We stand in silence, the sound of the wind filling our ears. The only person I've ever brought here was Mila. She understood my pain and was able to help me work through my grief. I never would've thought I would bring anyone else here and after we first met, I never would've thought that person would be Nash. I'm glad it's Nash.

"Do you want a moment alone?" he whispers in my ear.

Not taking my eyes off the picture of Jules and me, I nod and he kisses my head before walking back to the car. I crouch and rest one hand on her tombstone.

"A little bit of wind? That's all you've got? I finally bring a guy to meet you and you only respond with a little bit of wind? That seems underwhelming." I quietly laugh as I wait for something else to happen. When nothing does, I continue. "You know I wish you were here, but I'm still going to say it. I wish you were here. I wish I could introduce you to Nash and you two could swap embarrassing stories about me and I could pretend to be annoyed but secretly love that my sister and boyfriend are getting along."

I sniff and blink away the tears forming. "I wish I could spend months trying to find you the perfect present, only to get you something mediocre because I eventually ran out of time, and then you pretend to love it when we both know that isn't the case."

Closing my eyes, I inhale through my nose and exhale through my mouth. "I just wish you were here."

Looking over my shoulder, I make sure Nash is in the car and can't hear what I'm about to say.

I still speak in hushed tones as I lean in closer, "Want to know a secret? I think Nash may be the one. Like *the one* the one." I cover my smile with my hand. "How crazy is that? You and I always used to talk about getting married when we were older. What if that is a possibility for me now? Anyway, I'm about to get frostbite on my toes so this is goodbye for today. Merry Christmas, Jules, and I'll be looking for the sign. You know, the sign that tells me you love Nash and want him to be my husband."

I blow a kiss and laugh to myself as I walk away.

My feet stop the second the first white flake falls in front of my face. Slowly I look up to the sky and see that it's snowing. It's freaking snowing! Closing my eyes, I breathe in the smell of clean, fresh snow.

I turn back around. "That was a good sign, baby sister."

The second I step into the car, heat floods my entire body. I go to grab my seat belt when Nash places his hand on my knee.

"Are you all right?"

I sniff, buckle myself in, and turn my head to look at him. "It's snowing."

He furrows his brow in confusion. "Um, yeah?"

I giggle. "You don't get it. I asked her for a sign. I wanted to know if she liked you or not and now it's snowing."

Nash leans over to kiss my cheek. "It's snowing."

After we pull out of the cemetery, Nash drives me back to Market Square. He doesn't release my hand the entire drive and now my face hurts from smiling so much. He drops me off at Mila's abandoned car and meets me back at what is now Mila and Trey's place.

"Merry Christmas," I shout as Nash and I walk through the front door. The house is eerily quiet as we walk towards the living room.

"Are we early?" Nash whispers.

I shrug.

"Ahh!" I hear Mila shout and I pick up my pace. When I round the corner, Trey is on one knee and holding a small velvet black box. Mila is ugly crying as she jumps up and down. I hear the clink of Nash setting down the champagne we brought before I feel him wrap his hands around my waist.

"Emilia Cadence Grabowski," Trey says. "From the first day I met you, I had the biggest crush on you and convinced myself you wouldn't ever give me the time of day. You are my rock and my soulmate and my only regret is not getting down on one knee sooner. Would you—"

"Yes! Yes! Yes!" Mila screams.

"Let him finish," I tease.

Trey clears his throat. "Will you marry me?"

Mila's voice reaches an octave I think only opera singers can. She grabs Trey by the face and pulls him to a standing position before smashing his lips against hers. When they finally break, she's shaking with excitement. Trey guides the ring on her left hand and it fits perfectly, like it was always meant to be there.

"I guess it's a good thing we brought champagne," Nash says, kissing my temple. We all exchange hugs before Mila shoves her rock in my face. A white gold band with a huge—and I mean *huge*—single diamond in the center. Mila's entire face is flushed as she disappears to fix her makeup.

"Finally!" I say when I embrace Trey.

He shrugs. "What can I say? I had to save up for the right ring. I'm pretty positive she would've said yes regardless of what I got her, but Mila deserves the best."

I bump his hip with mine. "Yeah, she does!"

Much to my surprise, Trey has been planning his Christmas proposal for the past two months. Trey ordering Chinese food for dinner was obviously a ruse because he's made sure Mila's and his big night included an elaborate meal: filet mignon, baby potatoes, asparagus, Caesar salad, and cheesecake topped with strawberries. Nash and I say they should enjoy their moment and that we can let them have their privacy, but neither of them are having it.

"I made enough food," Trey says.

"I want to share this moment with my bestie and her boo. Now, sit your ass down or you can never borrow my car again," Mila threatens with a smile.

"I might not need it. Turns out I now have a BMW," I tease.

Nash clears his throat when Mila's eyes go wide. "Correction, I have a BMW, and Tatum has me."

Nash spends the meal trying to focus on the excitement of Mila and Trey's engagement, but all Mila wants to talk about is him.

"What kind of doctor are you? Where did you grow up? Is Tatum good in bed? Are you completely done being an asshole to my best friend? What's your favorite Christmas movie?"

Nash's grip on my thighs tightens with each question and I struggle to keep my laughter in. Mila has always been there for me and I suppose I deserve this. I put Trey through the wringer when I first met him. It's only fair. Nash passes Mila's "test" with flying colors and I kiss him as his prize.

Mila shrieks with happiness before raising her champagne flute.

She looks at each of us as she talks. "A toast. To my best friend for finding true love. To her boo for being the man she always needed. And to the love of my life. You are the most amazing person I have ever known and I can't wait to continue our lives together. You're stuck with me now, sucker!"

We all laugh as our glasses clink together. The bubbles explode in my mouth. I've never had expensive booze before, but I think I can get used to it. I am dating a doctor now.

"Hey, girlfriend?" Nash hollers from the kitchen. He and Trey opted to do the dishes while Mila and I cuddle on the couch to watch *A Christmas Story* on television.

"Yes, boyfriend," I shout back and Mila bumps my shoulder.

"Can you come here for a second?" His voice is getting softer, as if he's moving away from me. Pushing myself up from the couch, I go on my search. He's not in the kitchen anymore, so I continue to move through the house.

"Marco," I whisper.

"Polo," Nash mumbles from the direction of my old bedroom. During dinner, we told Mila and Trey our good news about moving in together. Mila was so excited that she jumped up from the table, almost knocking over her plate of food. We decided I'll start packing tomorrow.

I push open the door to find Nash lying on my old comforter. In only his boxer briefs.

"What do you think you're doing?" I giggle, leaning against the door frame as my eyes admire his insanely perfect body.

"You mentioned quite a few times how loud Mila and Trey are. How they've kept you up at night. How you saw Trey's bare ass due to their shower sex. What do you say we give them a taste of their own medicine?"

Stepping into the room, I shut the door behind me. Nash tosses his underwear at my feet and I pounce on top of him.

"Merry Christmas, my love."

Epilogue

"Sweetheart, please let me help you with that," Nash begs.

"I told you, I've got it!" I pant. "Just because my stomach is now abnormally large does not mean I can't carry a basket full of presents!"

"Excuse me, that perfectly sized belly is carrying my daughter." Nash kisses my temple, using the opportunity to pull the basket out of my hands. It's Christmas Day, exactly three hundred and sixty-six days since Nash and I officially got together and a lot has changed.

While I was busy helping Mila plan her wedding, I started feeling off. Turns out that was because I had a human being growing inside me! Being the impulsive and not sane people we are, after Nash and I found out we decided to get married. It was a small courthouse ceremony with shoes and a dress picked up at the mall a few blocks over, but it was perfect. Mom and Dad made the trip in their RV and I made sure to have a bouquet of yellow lilies in honor of Jules. Mila was my maid of honor and Nash and I exchanged rings under fluorescent lights that washed us both out. Though unconventional, August 4 will forever be one of my favorite days.

Mila's holding her front door open for us before we're even halfway up the driveway.

"Hurry! Get in here! It's freezing and I don't want my niece to come out as a popsicle!"

I roll my eyes. "That's not at all how that works."

Nash kisses Mila's cheek before walking into the house. Opening my arms wide, I hug Mila as tight as I can; the only problem is my belly is in the way, which causes us both to laugh. After shutting the door, Mila's hands find my belly.

"Will she kick for me? Little Mila has to know her Aunt Mila is here."

Laughing, I walk away from her and towards the kitchen. "As beautiful as your name is, we are not naming our daughter Mila."

"Did you tell her already?" Nash whispers through gritted teeth. I widen my eyes, trying to silently tell him to shut up.

"Tell her what?" Trey adds.

I hug Trey before walking over to Nash and swatting him on his perfectly shaped butt.

"Pregnancy has made this one a little horny," Nash teases before placing his arm around my shoulder and bringing me close to his body.

"Tell me what?" Mila demands.

Nash and I exchange a small kiss before I share. "Tell you that we have decided on a name."

Mila shrieks so loud that Trey walks over and places his hand over her mouth.

She must lick him because Trey rips his hand away and yells, "Gross!"

"Do you want to do the honors?" I ask Nash. Coming up with a name was a surprisingly agonizing task. For some reason, all the names we liked either had associations of being an ex or a horrible person or the name didn't fit with our preferred middle name. For example, Nash liked the name Sally, but I vetoed that immediately due to Sally Harris from fifth grade. Popular, a bully, and an all-around mean girl. No kid of mine will ever be named Sally.

Nash rubs his nose against mine before whispering, "You tell them."

Mila sighs, "Seriously, your old bedroom is still there, but I need to know the name before you go—"

"Don't tell them that!" Trey insists. "Last Christmas they were so loud, I thought the neighbors were going to call the cops."

"At least your fiancé didn't walk in and see my bare ass," Nash teases.

"Okay, okay!" I interrupt. "Baby girl's name is going to be—"

The doorbell interrupts us. I run to grab it because I've been waiting for this moment since last year.

I fling open the door to the smiling faces of my parents. They've been so busy lately but they promised to make it to Christmas dinner come hell or high water, according to my dad.

Hugs are exchanged and my mom oohs and ahhs over how grown up Mila is before she oohs and ahh over my belly.

"You're just in time," Nash says, kissing my mom's cheek and shaking my dad's hand.

"In time for what?" She sets down the veggie platter she brought, giving me a side hug due to my belly.

Everyone stares at me and I pause for dramatic effect, mainly because I know Mila is about to burst.

"We decided to name our baby girl Kira Juliette Anderson."

Nash and I kiss while Mila jumps up and down, clapping frantically. My mom wipes a tear away and my dad kisses my forehead.

"We're very proud of you," Dad says with a smile.

"Wait, I don't get it. Why the big reaction?" Trey asks. "I mean, it's a beautiful name, but ..."

Mila rolls her eyes, wiping the tears from her cheeks. "Jules was a nickname. Her sister's name is Juliette."

Trey's smile covers his entire face. "That's a beautiful name."

"It sure is," Mila whimpers. Trey laughs at her tears, pulling her into a hug.

After many hugs and many more tears are shared, Trey passes drinks around. Wine and beer for everyone but pregnant me. I opt for the sparkling grape juice Mila bought. She says she doesn't want me to feel left out and has Trey pour it into a champagne flute.

"Cheers to baby Anderson and potentially another little one on the way," Trey announces and my mouth drops open. My eyes find Mila's which are equally as confused.

"Not pregnant." She chuckles. "Just having a lot of fun." Mila winks as she bumps her hip into Trey's.

"Maybe we should eat and do presents soon. No offense, but seeing your ass once was enough for me," I joke.

"Why? His ass is spectacular," Mila says, grabbing a fist full of Trey's butt. Shaking his head in disapproval, he slides away from her.

"I feel like I'm missing something," my mom says, eagerly awaiting the gossip. My dad groans uncomfortably.

Nash clears his throat. "And cheers to my beautiful wife on her new publishing contract."

"You didn't tell me!" Mila clinks her glass to mine.

"Really? I can't wait to read your next one," Mom says.

Dad hugs me close. "Can the book be a thriller or something? Not that I didn't love the first one, but some activities should stay behind closed doors."

We all laugh as Dad mumbles, "I'm being serious."

Dinner consists of baked ham, sweet corn, bean casserole, mashed potatoes, and cranberries. And before you give all the credit to Trey and Mila for making such a fabulous and extravagant dinner, all they did was pick up the phone and place the order. No matter—the food is delicious and I justify eating three platefuls by saying baby Kira is hungry.

With help from Mila and Trey, I'm lowered to the floor and we all huddle around the Christmas tree. We exchange presents while Bing Crosby sings in the background. While Mila is drooling over the necklace Trey bought her, I take a moment to realize how much has changed over the past year and how I wouldn't change one thing about it. My parents visiting for the holidays is the cherry on top.

Looking up at my husband, his face aglow by the soft white lights on the tree, a smile crosses my face. My hand rests on my belly and my lips graze his. He places his hand on top of mine and whispers, "Merry Christmas, my love."